BINDAAS ZERO BOLLYWOOD HERO

N. Sampath Kumar is a novelist by night and an insomniac by day. He claims his physical body lives in Chennai; his astral body in the spiritual worlds. Delusions of grandeur seem to be his favourite hobby. That apart, he's been granted permanent residency status on Yahoo! Chess. After unleashing *Campus Cola* on the world, he bravely awaits your brutal feedback on his latest work at *sampathnovel@gmail.com* or *www.facebook.com/n. sampath.kumar*

BINDAAS
ZERO
BOLLYWOOD
HERO

N. SAMPATH KUMAR

RUPA

First published in 2012 by
Rupa Publications India Pvt. Ltd.
7/16, Ansari Road, Daryaganj,
New Delhi 110 002

Sales Centres:

Allahabad Bengaluru Chennai
Hyderabad Jaipur Kathmandu
Kolkata Mumbai

10 9 8 7 6 5 4 3 2 1

This novel is entirely a work of fiction. The names, characters, and
incidents portrayed in it are the work of the author's imagination.
Any resemblance to actual persons—living or dead—events or
localities is entirely coincidental.

To all those who are experiencing life as a movie;
and to all those who aren't

Contents

Main Cast

Vishnu aka Vishy	Protagonist
Usha	Vishy's ex-team leader and wife
Majumdar	Vishy's father
Kala	Vishy's mother
Bijlee	Vishy's childhood friend
Neelima	Vishy's childhood friend
Jana	Vishy's friend, philosopher and ex-colleague
Arpita	Vishy's former roommate and friend
Deepak aka Duniya	Owner of Cosmos Callways
Naveen	Ex-operations manager of Cosmos Callways
Harry	Producer–director of Vishy's first movie
Nimika	Vishy's first heroine
Bawa	Producer of Vishy's first movie
Harnoor	An ageing seductress
Javas	Extortionist
Pavan	Director of Vishy's unfinished movie

Kabi Bollywood's leading producer
Atul Kabi's son
Mizinah Kabi's mistress

Prologue

Xanadu Towers, 18th Road,
Bandra (West), Mumbai.
26 November 2011

Dear Reader,

I never thought marriage would be so tough. Here I am. Married to the only woman I've ever loved. And wondering if it was all worth it. Perhaps it was, at an emotional level. But at a professional level...? Your guess is as good as mine.

The basic problem is simple: a woman *thinks* with her heart and a man *feels* with his brain.

Should you or shouldn't you marry? I don't know. It works for some and others *pretend* that it's working for them.

Usha used to disagree with me on many things. Yeah, that's my wife. Funnily enough, her name means 'the dawn of hope'; but after marrying her, our life became the dusk of disaster. Thing is, I hadn't read her right despite having dated her for a year or so.

But this story isn't just about my marriage. It's the tale of my life: from confused teenager to confident call-centre agent to super-confident celeb.

I hope you will laugh and cry with me as I try a *Total Recall* of my story thus far. (Okay, I won't really mind if you don't cry, but do laugh at my expense.)

Love weighs heavily on my ego today—if I choose the former, I have to sacrifice the latter, and vice versa. Read on to find out how the cookie crumbled, folks.

Anyway, take care. Also, try not to marry, if you can resist the temptation. It's just not worth it.

Yours sincerely,

[signature]

PS: There are no chapters in this book, only levels, symbolic of how my success (or failure?) story moves from one level to the next... Sorry, got to go now, someone's at the door...

Could it be Usha having a change of heart? Ah, that would be heaven... 'Stop it, Vishy,' I tell myself as I move towards the darned door, propelled by hopeless hope. 'She's not going to come back to you, unless something miraculous happens...'

Now, why the hell do I feel like SRK in *Devdas*?

Escape from Alcatraz

*Boats are safe in the harbour—but
become quite bored there.*

Okay, let's begin by catching up with my life in Mayur Vihar, New Delhi, in the year 2008. I was a twenty-two-year-old, third-class graduate with a distance education degree in Commerce from DU. Plus, I was pretty clear that I wanted to escape from Delhi. For two reasons: (a) Dad and (b) Mom.

Here's why.

Dad would always tell me that I was a good-for-nothing lazy bum who didn't even have the skills to make a living as a boot polish boy.

Mom would take my side, saying that one day I would make it real big—so this stout maternal support created a pretty volatile situation at home.

When Dad would return from his super-intelligent bank job he would blow his top on seeing that I had purchased a new T-shirt or jeans.

Actually, our home should have carried a cautionary note saying 'Highly Inflammable'. Dad could have given microwave ovens a run for their money. He was forever in an angry mood, thanks to the fact that I had done horribly in Class XII...some four years ago. I had just scraped through the board exams, and couldn't join the prestigious colleges dotting North Campus or South Campus. To maintain my below-par academic record, I had also picked up quite a few arrears in the distance education course I had managed to get into, and dropped a year.

So then, for the past four years, Dad had assassinated my feelings systematically with infinite provocative statements made in my honour. Here's a sneak peek:

'You know, Kala, all my colleagues say that Vishy has proven that intelligence is not hereditary!'

'This boy should be sent to the zoo or the museum!'

'What did you feed him during his childhood? Stupidity or milk?'

'He's a chocolate face with a cabbage brain.'

I kept convincing myself that I would do something with my life to make Dad eat his words.

Thankfully, Dad was never physically violent with me. Perhaps because I was nearly double his size and my muscles stuck out rather threateningly from under the tight tees that were my regulation wear. But the tongue-lashings I got would have left lasting marks on the toughest of diamonds. Actually, they did leave painful scars on my heart and soul.

ॐ

As we—my friend Bijlee and I—were walking along the olive green pathways of Sanjay Jheel Park and admiring the scenery, I saw someone approaching from the opposite direction.

'Hey, isn't that Neelima?' wondered Bijlee.

'Hi...hmmph...guys!' said Neelima, halting beside us and smiling.

'Hi Neelu,' said Bijlee. 'I thought you jog only in the mornings.'

'Yeah...hmmph...but today was so nice...and...hmmph... drizzling slightly at four, so I decided to...' she broke off mid-sentence, seeing me looking away. 'Hey! What's the... hmmph...matter, Vishy? Can't you...hmmph...even say hi?'

'Arre,' explained Bijlee, 'he's sulking because his dad gave him some tight verbal slaps again—'

'I keep getting those all day...hmmph...and Mom says that no one will marry me if I resemble a road-roller... hmmph...but I'm not weak enough to let *that* spoil my mood,' said Neelima, provoking me.

She was a few years older than us, and her family was too uber-rich to worry about her academic performance— which, by the way, was worse than mine.

I remained silent and pretended to ogle the scenery.

She punched me on the shoulder. 'You know, you only look like a man...hmmph...but you have a woman's mind. Stop being a crybaby!'

'Enough of your nonsense, you don't know what I am going through, so just shut up! Talk to Bijlee, he's the hotshot IIT types!' I screamed.

Bijlee had got into IIT the previous year, on his third attempt, so he was the youth icon of our colony.

She put her arm around me, like a caring elder sis would.

'Vishy, you are a great guy and that's what counts in life!' she said.

'Yeah, everything evens out in the end—mark my words, you will make it real big one day,' said Bijlee.

'Yeah, I can see it in your eyes, Vishy! You are destined for great things, buddy,' cooed Neelima.

'Balls to the future *and* to your motivational talk! My mom keeps saying the same things and I am getting sick and tired of all these lies! I am a born loser, and am destined to die exactly as I was born!' I said.

'Vishy, we care for you more than you imagine,' Neelima said. 'Why don't you take up a job?'

'Go on. Rub Tata Salt into my wounds. I went to three interviews and they all humiliated me, making me wait for an hour and then saying my distance education degree can be used to make paper cones to sell peanuts. What can I do? I don't even know what I am good at—'

'Talking,' cut in Neelima. 'You are good at talking. You know, Arpi, my friend who flunked B.Com twice, she's working at a BPO in Pune. She's rocking there. Why don't you do the same? You'll do real well.'

'Oh, okay...hmmm...' I considered. 'Will they take me? Actually I'd love to go some place far from here. Pune sounds wonderful.'

Neelima immediately unzipped her trendy sweatshirt, and as Bijlee and I looked away politely, she pulled out her cell. Perhaps to talk to Arpita?

ᔛ

Now, you must be wondering why I am named after two of the most powerful gods running the cosmos. To know the answer, you need to understand some things about God-fearing people.

Such people are churned out someplace on the cosmic assembly line to devoutly worship some god or the other.

My dad worships Vishnu. My mom is a Shiva devotee. And she constantly cheeses him off by saying that her view of cosmology is the best.

They married in the summer of 1981, after much opposition from both families. They became vegetarians and also kept many vows, I am told, to placate their chosen gods. They survived the ruckus and engineered my arrival on the scene in 1986. Thus, I was named Vishnu Shankar. By the way, if I had turned out to be a daughter, I would have been named Lakshmi Parvati.

ॐ

'Here, speak to Arpita,' said Neelima, thrusting her cellphone into my hand.

'Hey, what do you mean? Give us an intro at least,' I said, refusing to take it.

'Yoohoo! *Arpiben, kemcho*,' trilled Neelima, turning on the speakerphone.

'Wow! Long time, Neelu! *Majja ma*! Howdy, girl!'

'Great! Listen, I want to ask you something. Is there a vacancy at your office for a guy from Delhi? Smart, graduate, damn good in English and all that...' said Neelima.

'Sure, who's he? Your boyfriend?' asked Arpita.

'Shut up! He's like my kid brother—his name is Vishy. Here, speak to him...' said Neelima.

'Hi, Ar...Arp...' I stuttered, wondering if addressing her as Arpi would seem too informal.

'Hey dude, it's cool, call me Arpi,' she said, reading my mind. So what do you do?'

'Nothing, Arpi, quite jobless...'

Would you like to be a telesales executive?' she said.

'Sure, sounds fun... What qualifications do they want?'

'Joblessness is the best qualification, Vishy.'

Where Eagles Dare

Money is the root cause of all snootiness.

A s I settled into my seat on the Nicejet flight to Pune, I felt like an eagle escaping from the shackles of a giant dinosaur. I even looked out of the window during lift-off to see if some giant killjoy Tyrannosaurus Rex would deposit our flight back on the runway.

My mind rewound to the conversation I had had with Dad last evening. It had been more of a sermon than a dialogue. He had said that I was going to Pune only to ruin myself further by getting involved in the murky world of drinks, drugs and dangerous damsels.

Mom had stayed stoically silent throughout his sermon, perhaps wondering if his prophecy would come true and hoping it wouldn't.

I took out a small family photograph from my wallet. It had been clicked about two years ago when Dad had got me a Canon digital camera from Singapore. I had carried this snap as a good-luck charm for my exams, badminton championships and even on my first date with a pimply but beautiful girl who'd seduced me into treating her to lunch at Soft Rock Café.

Bijlee knew about this photo fetish and had once said that my sentimental behaviour was quite contradictory to all the Dad-bashing I did in his presence.

'I hate my dad,' I'd said then to Bijlee, 'but that doesn't mean I don't love him.'

ॐ

Sounds trigger memories. The dull drone of the Boeing's engines catapulted me into the Karol Bagh of a distant past. Ah, nostalgia makes for a cruel companion. Memories travel faster than Phantom's eye can see—old jungle saying, or at least a tweak on the old jungle saying. And there was so much to remember...

Take, for instance, that Diwali evening when we decided to launch rockets horizontally on the road. Ooh, how the mad rocket had whizzed along that narrow gali and entered a passing Ambassador taxi from the front window and exited from the rear window! The dazed driver had managed to park the taxi and threatened to castrate us culprits, and thus make his radical barbaric contribution to India's population control programme...

How we had religiously burst 'atom' bombs, 'hydrogen' bombs and 'ladis' inside some twelve red postboxes standing majestically between Karol Bagh and West Patel Nagar...

Boy, how we had laughed when we learned that Kukka—the chronic womanizer—was suffering from an overdose of antibiotics after the doctor had advised him to take three tablets daily for a week to cure some sexually transmitted disease he had contracted at GB Road. Kukka had done some quick calculation, much like Suppandi in *Tinkle Digest*, and figured out that taking twenty-one tablets in one go would cure him of the itchy ailment in a single day, instead of a week...

Or how Mintoo had laid a bet with Chinu some four years ago that he would succeed in dating Dolly and Rinky simultaneously—two teenage bombs with the greatest knockers we had ever seen. One wintry afternoon, lucky Mintoo had also deflowered both and made our hormonal systems eternally envious...

Why was I feeling like a runaway bride fleeing rather disloyally from God knows what? You can't be emotionally wedded to the past or to your pals, can you?

※

'Sir, can I get you something?' The dulcet voice tore through the mists of the past and yanked me into the solid present.

'No, thanks,' I said to the air hostess, my eyes involuntarily going to her inviting cleavage.

'Sure, Sir?' she tried again.

'No, thanks, I have some eats in my bag,' I assured her and the lady on my left glanced at me as if I was some village bumpkin who ought to be travelling by the Jhelum Express, instead of Flight NG 287. She made faces, as if expecting me to boorishly wolf down oily puris, aloo subzi, aachar and stuff.

I didn't disappoint her. I reached out for my duffel bag in the overhead locker, pulled out a greasy cellophane-secured packet containing Mom-made aloo and mooli paranthas, settled into my seat, and chomped loudly to spoil her breakfast. I even burped thrice to get her grimacing.

I hate snootiness more than anything else.

As Good as it Gets

Generosity is the greatest sign of an evolved being.

The autorickshaw snaked through more potholes than roads as it noisily zoomed towards Arpita's pad in Goratown Park. Since it had been raining like crazy, it felt like we were water-skiing on a sea of boulders and craters disguised as roads.

I kept requesting the autorickshaw driver to slow down as he clutch-braked-clutch-braked feverishly, skidding and outmanoeuvring millions of other miracles on wheels or legs.

He kept turning back, constantly reassuring my frazzled nerves, saying, 'No worry, Saab. Me expert. You relax,' and continued with his James Bond-esque driving expertise, which did everything except make me feel relaxed.

But he was a good bloke. He warned me about bird flu and AIDS, and also told me which places to avoid going to, and where to find cheap but good grub even after midnight.

'But be careful of Pune girls, Saab, most of them just want to do masti with your money,' he said, reminding me of Dad. 'Youth isn't meant for sex but for making a career for yourself' reminded me of Bijlee. 'Lots of foreign maals where you are going to stay, and they are all full of love' reminded me of Kukka.

'That's Buddha Bakery, Saab,' he said, pointing to the left, 'and just beyond on the right, if you take that street, you have the Taozen ashram. All very costly, Saab...'

I tried to shake off my loved ones from my mind and resisted the temptation of calling up anyone. Though I did text Mom to say that I had reached safely. Had I? The way he was driving, throwing caution and auto simultaneously to the winds, made me seriously wonder if I should delete 'safely' from the text. But it had already been sent.

శ్రీ

Beyond a huge green municipality bin brimming with discarded plastic bags and buzzing houseflies was Famous Heights II, Arpita's pad.

As I heaved a sigh of relief that we had made it in one piece, settled the fare and stepped out of the auto, someone smiled at me. I smiled back and the stranger approached me. His long beard, pyjama slacks and grey T-shirt looked as if they hadn't been washed in ages.

'New? Welcome. Need flat? Decent, semi-decent? Independent, 7,000. Sharing, 3,000–4,000. Myself Swami Keerti. Yourself?' said the friendly stranger, extending his calloused hand.

'Myself Vishy. Thanks, but I am going to stay with a friend,' I said, avoiding shaking his hand by pretending to search for something in my duffel bag.

'No problem,' he said, flashing a tobacco-stained grin. 'Maybe later you needing me. Here, take my card.'

I took the card gingerly.

'Who friend? Tell me, I know all here. You just say Swami Keerti's friend and they all rushing to help you. Which flat?'

'202,' I said, hoping he would leave me alone.

'Ah, Ma Prema Leela, nice, loving girl, very helpful person, my friend too,' he said.

'Huh? My friend is Arpita Desai,' I said. 'You are making a mistake—'

'Arre, we sanyasis no mistake making. We are perfect, almost God,' he grinned. 'That is her sanyas name.'

'What is sanyas name?'

'Oho, all Taozen sanyasis have new names. So you break away from past, live moment to moment and get enlightened, just like Master. New names mean new life, new friends, new joys, new celebrations. Understanding?'

'Yes, yes,' I said, lifting my suitcase as he pointed to a moss-covered path that would hopefully lead to Arpita's flat.

ॐ

'Yoohoo! Vishy! Welcome, welcome!' trilled Arpita as she opened the door and gathered me in her arms.

I certainly wasn't prepared for this robust greeting by someone I barely knew, or for what I saw. Arpita was wearing an almost see-through red robe and I could clearly make out that she wasn't even wearing a bra as she gave me a tight hug. I mumbled something that sounded like a thankful grunt, and she laughed.

'Buddy, it's a braless Sunday!' she said, somehow reading my thoughts and discomfiture.

I couldn't take my eyes off her voluptuous body and amazingly beautiful face. Her blue–green eyes twinkled mischievously every time she caught me looking at her.

'This is where I usually sit, as it overlooks the Burning Ghat. That's the local crematorium, and you'll meet all kinds of crazy people there—from madmen to geniuses. I'll take you there in a while,' she said, pointing out the sights from a balcony covered with pigeon droppings, discarded cigarette butts and rusty cans of Budweiser, Foster's and Heineken.

She was presenting the yucky scenery to me as if it were the Mughal Gardens.

'Nice,' I lied.

'Beer?' she offered, pulling out a can from her refrigerator.

'Sorry, I don't drink,' I explained. 'Water will do.'

'Oh, why be sorry about it? I gather you don't smoke either?'

'No, I don't.'

'Good, but I am toh baba addicted to both, if you don't mind.'

'I don't. It's your place, your life, and who am I to—'

'*Our* place.'

'Okay, thanks for being so welcoming—'

'Fuck the formalities, Vishy the Rishi. That rhymes so well, na?'

'Yeah.'

'Okay, you want to take a wash? Switch on the geyser if you wish to.'

'Not now, later. You stay alone here?'

'Now, yes. Earlier I had this friend, Payal, who has now been transferred to Bangalore, so we have the entire flat to ourselves. Your room was Payal's—you can remove the Tom Cruise and Salman Khan posters if you wish.'

'No, no, let it be. I'll be here for only a brief while—'

'Why?'

'I mean I'll soon need to look for a place for myself, na?'

'Why? You uncomfortable with me already?'

'Arre, no, Arpi, I didn't mean it that way—I meant you'd also like to have some space to yourself, right?'

'Not at all. I have my room for that. You aren't going anywhere, honey!'

'Okay, then I'd like to chip in with the rent.'

'We will discuss all that later, Vishy, after you start making some money, okay?'

'Cool!'

'Now just make yourself feel at home.'

'Oh, thanks. Frankly, I didn't expect such a warm welcome.'

'Or a braless one. The world is full of surprises, isn't it?'

'You bet.'

ॐ

Buddha Bakery was a gaggle of sorts. And the 'bakery' bit was a clear misnomer. It was more of an open-air eatery than a cake shop and nearly spilled over onto the main road. The ambient noise would have put the Kumbh Mela in the shade. What struck me as fairly intriguing was that almost no one was ogling the ladies in skimpy clothes or transparent robes, through which you could nearly read the brand of their undergarments.

The eatery was jam-packed and bursting at the seams. After a while, the collective din got to me and I asked Arpita if earmuffs shouldn't be part of the menu.

'Sunday evenings are hugely crowded. Almost the entire Pune descends here,' explained Arpita.

She was saying a million 'hellos' every minute, and embracing and cheek-pecking so many Taozen guys and girls that I wondered if she was some kind of hugging-and-kissing machine.

'You seem to know nearly everyone here,' I said.

'Yeah... Oh, by the way, you still a virgin?'

Her question sent a minor shockwave rippling through me.

'Hey, c'mon,' she prodded, 'if you want to be a good telesales executive, then you ought to open up a bit.'

'Well, take a wild guess, Arpi,' I said.

'Hmmm...' she said, sizing me up. 'I'd say you have kissed a girl but have never made love to one, right?'

'Wrong and right. Never kissed. Never slept,' I said.

'Aha!' she said. 'Total chikna, fresh maal, huh?'

'Now stop making me feel so conscious,' I said.

'Okay, want to take a walk to Burning Ghat? The lights reflecting on the river will be a great sight now. Perhaps we'll even bump into someone interesting,' she said.

'Sure,' I mumbled, dying to get away from the madding crowd I had tolerated for close to three hours.

LEVEL 4

The Firm

All sales talks are sophisticated lies
projected as simple truths.

Cosmos Callways was a sprawling call centre located on the fifth floor of a huge commercial complex called Success Storyz on Sepoy Gokhale Road. The garish yellow reception desk was shaped like a huge, flattened landline telephone.

'Meet Shalini, the centre of our call centre, she's the nucleus around which our entire business revolves,' said Arpita, introducing me to the receptionist.

Shalini stood up in greeting. Her perfume teased, skimpy skirt titillated, tank top invited, lavender lipstick seduced and cute mascara-enhanced eyelids hypnotized. I struggled to stop staring at this scorcher. But somehow I smiled dignifiedly and managed to maintain my composure (a tough task for a sex-starved virgin), while Arpita grinned knowingly.

'Shalu to you,' the girl said, and looking at Arpita, 'Your friend?'

'Hmmm, you could say that. Vishy's going to work with us, so you guys will be seeing lots of each other in the near future,' said Arpita.

'Ooh, I hope you don't mean that *literally*—though I wouldn't mind that,' cooed Shalini, and both ladies laughed loudly.

I missed the joke.

'Arpi, Duniya has left a message for you—I guess he's coming by the afternoon flight. You will need to reach the Meridien around four for some meeting,' Shalini continued.

'Oh, great, he must be coming with some stupid firang clients in tow. You know, the last time, I was listening to silly jokes and watching card tricks. *Kya karein, karna padta hai...*' said Arpita.

'*Haan, jhelna toh padega, paapi pet ka sawaal hai*,' agreed Shalini.

'Who's Duniya?' I asked.

'That's our owner, Deepak Rastogi's nickname. Since our world and happiness revolves around him, we fondly call him Duniya. Nice guy actually...' said Arpita to me, and turning to Shalini, 'Okay, nucleus, many interviews today, send the good-looking guys to me, and the rest to Usha...'

'You've already ensnared a handsome hunk, doll, stop being greedy,' ribbed Shalini, throwing a saale-tu-toh-phas-gaya look at me.

I blushed as the ladies winked at each other.

᠅

'You can take this as an official interview,' she said, 'and I don't care a damn if you are Arpi's friend.'

'Yeah, sure,' I said.

'No slang, please.'

'Sorry?'

'*Yeah* is slang. I'd suggest you say "yes". Piece of advice: we service British customers, so your English better be real prim and propah, okay?'

'Yeah... Sorry, yes...'

'Good. I can see that you are a quick learner.'

'Thanks.'

'Is this your resumé?' she asked, glancing derisively at the Microsoft Word printout I'd got rather hastily done from a cybercafé the previous evening.

Shucks! Why hadn't Arpita warned me about this? She had coached me a bit, yes, but this interview was like facing a frigging one-woman execution squad.

The only saving grace was that she was gorgeous—90 per cent Juhi Chawla, 10 per cent Raveena Tandon, said my biocomputer—and you can call me a masochist, but I was kind of beginning to enjoy being grilled thus by this stunner.

If I had a lustometer on me, it would have graded the three babes who had impacted me the most in the past twenty-four hours thus: Usha>Shalini>Arpita.

'Yes, I hope everything is right with my biodata,' I said.

'Balls! You never call a resumé a biodata! God, do you have any idea how downmarket that sounds?' she thundered, slapping the two sheets on her table.

'Oh, okay, sorry about that, I thought they were acceptable synonyms...'

'Stop apologizing. It's a sign of weakness. Hmmm... school...what is this? BIDES, Mandir Marg, New Delhi?'

'Huh? That is my school.'

'It still *is* your school?'

'I mean...I mean, was...'

'And what would it expand into?'

'Expand? Maybe it would expand into a college someday, if they decide to—'

'I am asking what does BIDES mean?'

'Oh, that? That is Bengali Indian Divine Education Society.'

'Is that why your English is so tacky? You guys learnt things in Bengali?'

'No, Madam, it is an English medium school—'

'Usha. That's my name. And madams run brothels, not call centres. We are all on first-name basis here. No sirs, no madams, got it?'

'Okay.'

'So why have you come here all the way from Delhi? I am sure there are many good call centres there.'

'Well, to tell you the truth, I wanted to stay away from my parents and all.'

'All right, now we will play a game.'

'Okay... '

'Pretend that you are a salesman and I am a bald man named Mr MacLean. Now you have to sell me a comb. How will you do it?'

'Huh?'

'C'mon, give it a shot. Think of something. And do it fast.'

So she pretended to be a customer; and I acted the role of a confident salesman on a mock call for about three minutes. I didn't know if Usha liked my sales talk or not—she hardly smiled or appreciated anything. Was her face made of rigid iron, instead of flexible muscles and responsive skin?

॰

Arpita had left to meet Duniya and the visiting firangs, where she had to make a presentation about the workings of Cosmos Callways. She had said that her presentation would hopefully help her rope in new clients looking to outsource their credit cards and home loans business to us. 'Us' meant a huge English-speaking Indian workforce willing to work at hourly rates that would be considered peanuts back in the UK.

I wasn't complaining though, as call centres mushrooming all over the countryside were the new haven (or heaven) for academic non-performers like me.

Talking of academic losers, there were quite a few of us waiting at the terrace of Cosmos Callways, which overlooked a huge Durga temple below. One girl sitting at the table behind mine was crying. She was being consoled by self-styled counsellors.

I leaned back in my chair and cradled my neck in my palms, as if to sort out a crick, so that I could take in more of the conversation. 'That bloody bitch...she...' I heard the crybaby saying, 'she said I should re-enter kindergarten...' (Surely she was referring to Usha).

'Why?' asked a girl, pretending to be concerned.

'She...she...asked me to recite some nursery rhymes,' sobbed the girl, perhaps dabbing her eyes, 'and I couldn't remember any.'

'Not even "Jack and Jill"?' asked another, quite aghast.

'No, I was too nervous,' said the tragedy queen.

'Forget it! It's okay, come, let's have a juice...' said someone.

Bloody hell, I remembered at least ten nursery rhymes! But Usha hadn't asked me anything as simple as that.

Thankfully, the peons began distributing the results, so the irksome chatter petered out into a studied silence. Everyone began scrutinizing the forms that would decide the levels of their present self-worth and future remuneration.

Anyway, I made it.

LEVEL 5

The Saint

We usually learn about ourselves from our opposites.

I had nearly a week to kill before I was conscripted for the training programme. A day after I had proudly inked the appointment letter, I took a morning walk to the Burning Ghat. One pyre was still burning—covered with a huge asbestos sheet—and someone was trying to light his beedi with a burning ember from it.

Something about him intrigued me. His steel-rimmed spectacles, long mane, lush beard, gangly frame and the way he held his neck, as if proud of his clearly humble circumstances, made him look as majestic as a king...or an arrogant scientist. Actually, he looked more like a Mughal emperor who had relinquished his throne recently and settled in a hut, as if to announce that true royalty didn't consist of owning a palace, but of owning oneself. This must be that 'Einstein in a long kurta' Arpi had once told me about.

'Hi,' I said as I sat next to him at the edge of the half-burnt pyre, unable to contain my curiosity about him any longer.

'Getting bored?' he asked.

'Yes, totally bored,' I said. 'They call me Vishy!'

'They call me insane,' he said.

'But you aren't,' I replied.

He turned towards me, his eyes glinting. I will never forget the deep, mysterious pools of optical brilliance that had a devastating effect on me. I had never seen eyes like these—soft, languid, clear, relaxed, honest and enigmatic, as if they had seen all that was worth seeing and knew all that was worth knowing. I couldn't look into his eyes for too long. It was as if they could read through me and pluck out my deepest thoughts.

I became uneasy and hastily went and sat on the park bench.

He let me be, and continued to smoke beedis, looking at the grey ash, which had once been a walking-talking being. I shuddered, thinking that I, too, would one day end up on such a pyre. I wondered if my burnt remains would also function as a lighter, to symbolize that finally I had been of some use to society, albeit late (pun intended).

Ten minutes passed, and I felt increasingly guilty for having disengaged from him so abruptly. But his eyes—there was something about them that I just couldn't take.

'Sorry,' I said from behind him after a while.

'About what?' he asked, still looking at the pyre.

'Well, for having insulted you, for having walked away,' I explained.

'Nobody can insult me without my consent. And I haven't given you mine,' he said matter-of-factly.

'Didn't it bother you? My abrupt behaviour, I mean?' I asked.

'Not at all. Why should someone's emotions and reactions affect me? Am I a slave to your behavioural patterns?' he said, quite surprised that I had expected him to feel hurt.

'Cool, actually I couldn't look into your eyes,' I explained.

'Understandable. They are the eyes of truth. The world of deceit can't face them for too long,' he replied.

'My friend says you haven't spoken to anyone for the past month.'

'I haven't.'

'Why?'

'Information should be given on a qualified-to-know basis. And right now, you aren't qualified to know.'

'Tea?' I finally asked, eager to shift conversational gears and location. 'I would like to have some kandha poha and vada pav too. Famished. Would you like to join me?'

'Sure,' he said. 'I haven't had any food for three days now.'

༄

Over the next five days, I learnt much about him. How he had been defrauded of his inheritance by his stepmother and her sons after his dad died intestate, two years ago. He had trustingly signed some no-objection clause on a stamp paper and they had coolly denied him his share. It ran into crores of rupees, but he didn't seem too perturbed about it. He said that he had had an enlightenment experience after that, and all the money in the world paled in comparison to what he had gained last summer.

He'd been living in Mumbai when his stepmom had turfed him out, and when he had run out of money, he worked as a steward in some restaurants, an insurance salesman, a pizza delivery boy, a chauffeur and a receptionist at a hotel. The funny part was that he was a qualified software engineer (six years my senior, actually) but had tired of computers, programming and such stuff.

'After my enlightenment, I didn't like to do jobs where I had to apply my mind—somehow I just couldn't continue in my job as a software developer, since my mind had expanded to a supra-mental plane. But the blue-collar stuff, anything physical, suited me just fine. I guess now I am a bit more settled in my mind—it is a shattering experience,' he said.

We went on long walks, past the Buddha Bakery, past all the chatter, breaking our journey every now and then to have tea or dabelis, past a five-star hotel, which, he said, was 'just an air-conditioned prison for the elite, because real life is under the raw skies', past the bridge, past the railway lines and into the Pune railway station.

We sat for hours watching trains settling into the station or preparing to chug away slowly. Trains fascinated him. He talked a lot about how so-called lifelong relationships, with parents, lovers, friends or anyone, would all get de-linked, just like coaches do at railway yards, as everyone would eventually disappear into the fabric of another existence, in another dimension. He said one should neither love nor be attached to any person, place or thing.

Naturally, he did most of the talking. His logic and strange points of view were music to my ears. I became attached to him, despite his cautionary note on the subject of relationships.

He had even told me his name: Janardhanan Murthy. But it took him quite a while to reveal that. I kept asking him if it was some kind of state secret. He kept rebuking me for snooping around.

Perhaps I was the only one in Goratown Park who knew his real name. The kids in the shanty next to the ghat called him 'Pagal Baba', but he didn't seem to mind. The adults kept a respectful distance and he said that that suited him just fine. I asked him after a few days if I could call him Jana and he said, quite uncharacteristically, that it sounded 'pretty cute and sweet'.

I had found a companion far more intelligent than Bijlee, far more humane than Arpita and far more caring than Neelima.

When I asked him what 'enlightenment' was all about, he just looked at the sky in silence.

'Hey, I asked you something,' I said.

'Who is asking?' he said.

'Me, who else?'

'Then you can never get enlightened.'

'What do you mean?'

'The *I* in you can never get enlightened. It is only when the *me* vanishes that enlightenment happens.'

LEVEL 6

Private Lessons

Everything is hard before it becomes easy.

At office, we trainees were divided into two groups of twenty each. I tried my best to get into Arpita's group but was given the same 'professional ethics' funda. Damn! Three weeks with Usha would be hell. Anyway, the sixteen grand at the end of it all should be ample recompense for a battered ego, I thought in a bid to console myself.

'Okay, class, now that the introductions are done with, I'd like to begin by asking you a simple question. What is a telephone?' asked Usha.

Nineteen hands went up. I didn't raise mine.

'Why, Vishy? Am I asking a very difficult question, or do you think you are too bright for such a simple query?' she thundered.

'Well, Usha, the query isn't difficult, so simply put, there ought to be a catch to it...and it takes great wisdom to hide your wisdom,' I retorted, visibly angry.

The class was impressed. Usha wasn't.

'Aha, we have a smart alec here. That's not your line. It's an ancient quote,' she said.

'Just goes to prove that my line was stolen even before I was born,' I retorted.

'Okay, Vishy, since you are such a smartass, define "telephone",' she challenged.

'A telephone is an instrument that facilitates long-distance communication,' I replied tiredly.

'Wrong,' she said.

'Then?' asked Priya. 'He seems right.'

'Dumbo, when I ask a question, I don't want a *literal* answer. Even a KG student knows what a telephone is. I am looking for a *symbolic* answer—like what a telephone means to *you*.'

'Oh, for me, it means I can talk to my boyfriend till late in the night without the fear of getting caught,' said Maureen airily.

Usha glared at her for a while, obviously not liking the definition.

'The telephone, for you all, is your bread and butter from today onwards. The telephone will make or mar your career. The telephone is your god—it will *create* your future. Got it?' said Usha.

Nineteen heads nodded assent.

The entire training session went on the same way, with Usha asking questions, making us feel like illiterate bacteria and answering the questions herself...

∿

'Arpi, I have a surprise for you,' I said the following Sunday, as I was readying a breakfast of cheese omelettes and bread.

'What's the surprise, Vishy dear? Lost your virginity finally?' she asked.

'I've been hanging out with the Einstein in the long kurta,' I said triumphantly.

'Really? How on earth did you manage that? He seems so reticent!'

'Well, while you were busy with the recruitment drive and all, I succeeded in befriending him...'

'Great! Tell me about him. I'm sure there's more to him than meets the casual eye.'

So I told her everything except the software engineering part—Jana had made me swear on my job that I wouldn't divulge that to anyone, for whatever reason. Arpita was clearly surprised that he spoke chaste English and claimed to be enlightened. She asked me to go to the Burning Ghat and invite him over for breakfast, and I said that he might clam up, thinking that we were coming on too strong. I promised, however, to introduce her to him at a neutral venue like the bakery in the evening (she'd stopped visiting the ghat two days ago, ever since some new eve-teasing squatters had stalked her there). Arpita gets magnetically drawn to two kinds of people—madmen and mystics. Perhaps Jana was a bit of both?

༄

'Shall we go to the bakery?' I asked Jana later in the evening, slightly guilty that I was conning him into meeting Arpita.

'No, too crowded on a Sunday evening. Some other time,' said Jana.

'Cool,' I said, relieved that I hadn't succeeded in deceiving him.

'So how's your training coming along? Enjoying it?' asked Jana.

'Bull! It is mandatory and the trainer is one helluva sadist!'

'Girl?'

'Yeah, and quite a bomb too!'

'Well, it's good to interact with sadists. Teaches you a lot about your tolerance levels, doesn't it?'

'You bet!' I retorted sarcastically.

'Well, Vishy, life is all about the capacity to endure pain. All great men throughout history have had a phenomenal ability to absorb pain, both physical and mental.'

'Then I am surely not great, Jana, because I just hate the way that bitch makes us feel like vermin.'

'Have respect for gurus, Vishy, there's a lot to learn, even from the worst.'

'Fuck it. Let's go to Utsav for a bite.'

ॐ

After understanding tough English phrases, it was time to master the history, geography and civics of the UK. By the end of the second week, we perhaps knew more about the UK than its own population.

Usha warned us that the toughest part would be process training, which was slated to raise its ugly head in the third week. This was to be followed by a test of nerves and skill, both in written and oral format, failing which meant getting the pink slip and the jobless blues.

Me, I had practised well with Jana—I had made him read all my notes and printouts every evening, and you know what, Jana had mastered all of it better than me!

What a pro! I used to joke with him that he could join Cosmos Callways as a trainer, immediately.

꒰꒱

The second week of training naturally ended on a Saturday, and even as most of us made plans to go to the movies, Arpita burst in on our session with an animated announcement.

'Guys, I hope you all are having a good time. Well, we have a small situation. Four people from my batch have left and have not been seen for two days now!'

'Oh, this has queered your pitch,' said Usha. (Did I see a vamp-like glint in her eyes?)

'Yeah,' trilled Arpita nervously. 'So, if any of you can recommend a few friends, then we can train them quickly to keep the numbers. To motivate you, Cosmos plans to give you guys a whopping 5,000 bucks for any of your pals selected for our process... Oh, and Usha, two members from your team will be joining mine for now.'

Usha's face fell.

The rest of the class beamed silently.

'Thanks,' said Arpita, but added a caveat immediately. 'You get the money provided your friends work with us for at least six months. Can you folks do it?'

A few guys and girls said they could, and I had already decided what to do.

I declined the movie invite as the training session ended, and headed straight for the Burning Ghat.

ॐ

Jana was sitting by a burning pyre, smoking beedis as usual. How very predictable he had become.

'Hey, dude,' I said. 'I have super news!'

'You've attained nirvana?' he made a jibe.

'Nothing as grand and spiritual. I have a plan for us to make some material progress, some quick, easy money.'

He seemed least interested as I explained the sudden requirement caused at Cosmos by new recruits who were playing hookey. I tried seducing him by promising to share half the promised ₹5,000 with him after six months. I told him the place had great babes, free snacks, food and coffee, but he just wouldn't budge.

'Listen, Vishy, I just want to *be*, as of now.'

'Dude, *please*, do this as a favour to me, you know I get so bored out there with all those cretins floating around. With you around, it will seem like a picnic. Please, Jana, please, let's do this! God knows, you and I need the money. How long can you live like this? *I need you with me!*'

There is one good thing about compassionate people. They respond well to pleas. If you implore them in the right tone, they are gullible enough to let you have your way.

'Okay, what do I have to do?' he asked.

'Nothing, Jana, just fucking absolutely nothing! You already know most of the stuff. Process training is about to begin the day after. I'm sure they will lap you up. Leave it all to me. We will just need to get your beard out of the way and—'

'Balls! No way am I shaving off my beard!'

'Hey, Jana, it is not Samson's locks holding enormous power. Cosmos has a rule against beards. French beards and moustaches are allowed.'

He listened quietly as I grovelled and pleaded, and finally relented, agreeing to let me buy him trousers, shirts, socks and shoes when I said that he could return the money after he got his first salary from Cosmos.

～

Arpita bumped into us at 10 p.m. at Buddha Bakery after Jana and I had shored up his wardrobe at Pune Central.

She didn't recognize him at first, what with his clean-shaven dapper looks, distinguished casuals and cropped hair.

'Hi Arpi,' I said, sipping the ABC juice and pointing at Jana. 'Recognize him?'

'No, sorry, someone from Usha's group?' she asked quizzically. 'Seems slightly familiar.'

'But I do know that you are Arpita Desai, and you even brought me biscuits and burgers on many evenings, thank you...though I chose not to speak with you then,' smiled Jana.

'Evenings? You mean at the Burning Ghat? Ooh, the Einstein in the long kurta!' she screamed, recognizing his horn-rimmed spectacles.

'You are quite perspicacious, aren't you?' laughed Jana.

'Wow! My, my! You do look handsome,' said Arpita, extending her hand. 'Nice vocab too... Call me Arpi.'

'And Vishy has christened me Jana,' he said.

'I know... So what's with the new look, Jana?'

'Well, take a wild guess! He is my passport to the 5,000 bucks you promised earlier today!' I said.

'Omigod! You are going to join Cosmos Callways?' she asked him.

'Only if I get through your famed rigorous screening procedure,' smiled Jana.

'He knows so much, Arpi, that you'd recruit him right away—knows about the training stuff, I mean. In fact, he's the one who helped me mug up all the notes,' I said excitedly.

'Really?' she queried.

'Yeah, ask him anything. Bet you a cheese omelette he'll come up trumps,' I said confidently as I signalled to the waiter to get her an ABC.

'Game?' she asked Jana.

'Sure, shoot,' he said sportingly.

'Where in the UK can the queen never go to?'

'House of Commons.'

'Pronounce E-d-i-n-b-u-r-g-h.'

'Edin-bur-rah.'

She asked him some twenty-odd trick questions, and he was bang on all the time.

'My bust size?' she finally asked.

'38, I'd imagine,' he said confidently.

'Fuck, Jana! How on earth did you get *that* right? So uncanny! You know quite a bit! You will be a threat to us trainers!' she cooed appreciatively.

'See? What did I tell you?' I said triumphantly. 'Is he on?'

'Full-on, buddy, full-on!' she said excitedly. 'Go screw Usha's trip at the interview—she has finally met her match!'

'Arpi, can Jana check into our flat? He will also share the rent after he gets his salary,' I said.

'Sure, he's most welcome, the more the merrier,' she replied cheerfully. 'Jana, you are amazing!'

'That is an understatement!' he said laughingly.

The Man Who Knew Too Much

Be happy even when you lose,
because someone has won.

I made the first sale in my group in an unforgettable trial run on a Saturday, and rang the small bell that we were supposed to clang—the sonic equivalent of a victory lap?

What ecstasy! It was compounded by the fact that Usha gave me a tight hug.

But good feelings never last too long. Mine lasted for just an hour and three-quarters. Nobody had succeeded in making a single sale after mine, despite all of us making some four hundred calls.

All that was about to change.

Usha was sulking and shaking her head every now and then, saying, 'You guys are just burning the hot leads database.'

I looked towards Jana. He had closed his eyes and seemed to be intently listening to something. But for his tense concentration, and the way his neck muscles became tauter by the minute, you'd have thought he was calmly meditating. I sidled closer and could hear some Western classical music wafting from his headset.

'What the fuck?' I whispered to Jana and he shushed me.

'Mr Farrell, that's definitely Beethoven's "Moonlight Sonata", said Jana.

I looked on, amazed, and signalled to Usha that I was taking a break. I plugged off my headset and tuned into Jana's call.

'...the ways of life are strange indeed...' said Mr Farrell. 'It is so ironic that God should make a music composer deaf... Anyway, let's continue...'

'Hmm...' said Jana. 'This one is "The Marriage of Figaro" by Mozart...'

For the next ten minutes, Mr Farrell played several musical pieces on his system, and Jana identified each symphony correctly. Was this a marketing call or a quiz show?

As Jana ended the call and clanged the bell rather smugly, Usha screamed, 'Okay, all, log off immediately after you finish your present calls! This is a record at Cosmos! *Ten sales in one call*! Amazing! Ten hugs to Jana!'

She gathered him in her arms and Jana pretended to be happy. I could read his pretence as I looked into his eyes. There are few people who hate to succeed, but Jana was one of them. For him, success was a kind of existential poison that he wanted to avoid desperately—perhaps success was anathema to spiritualists?

'How did you manage *ten*, Jana?' asked Usha, still entwined around him like a hungry octopus.

'Well, Mr Farrell said that if I could identify the composers of some symphonies, then he'd be willing to buy ten for his ad agency...'

'People,' continued Usha, 'give a big hand to Jana! And clap till your palms hurt!'

The focus had shifted from me. From a hero, I had become a zero in the span of a hundred minutes.

I looked away, my entire frame shaking with jealousy and anger.

At the end of the shift, our whiteboard showed that I was second to Jana. We had beaten Arpita's team 19–2, though.

༈

The following weekend, we sat listening to Arpita's corporate woes.

Arpita loved discussing things with Jana because (a) he was the Mr Know-All of our gang and (b) he gave her 'high-spirited' company by guzzling dozens of beers, even while puffing away on umpteen packets of cigarettes.

Our balcony seemed to be a cross between a partially open gas chamber and a desi daru ka adda.

'Naveen Katyal will return tomorrow,' said Arpita.

'Who's that?' I asked.

'Our operations manager and immediate boss. He was in the UK on business. The grapevine has it that he has a soft spot for Usha. Perhaps they are seeing each other...'

'Someone's personal life is none of our business,' said Jana as I felt a strange knot of envy and possessiveness hit the pit of my stomach. Usha on my mind and heart was not a pleasant feeling on a relaxed Sunday evening, especially when there seemed to be a more successful, more powerful man in her life.

'Don't be naïve, Jana, personal life affects corporate life. Right now I am neck and neck with Usha but she could upstage me and become a team manager...' griped Arpita.

'So you would have to report to her if that happens?' I asked.

'Of course!' snapped Arpita.

'Arre, Arpi, life is too short to worry about competing with or out-ranking anyone, let things unfold as they will,' consoled Jana.

'That's easy for you to say. I have slogged my ovaries off for this company. I can't let an opportunity slip by, just because Miss Usha Tripathi is playing footsie with a creep like Naveen,' she said.

'So what can you do about it?' I asked.

'I don't know,' she said, sighing deeply, and the vigorous inhalation made her cough a bit.

'Don't worry,' said Jana. 'Existence will find a way to make you race ahead of her. Life always moves in favour of kind hearts.'

'You are such a soothing, darling sounding board, Jana,' cooed Arpita.

He smiled at that, and I excused myself by feigning drowsiness as my eyes had begun watering because of all the smoke.

Plus, they were now exhaling senti dialogues, which I find quite intolerable, especially when it is the alcohol that does most of the talking at such times.

The Great Dictator

Teaching is learning twice.

Naveen Katyal was a helluva pompous ass. He ordered all of us into a training room that could barely seat twenty. So, most of us were standing like star-struck commoners, peppering the rear of a seedy cinema hall in a film-crazy small town. He didn't even apologize to the standees for the inconvenience.

'Okay, team, you all know that I am the ops manager. Nice meeting you guys. Now, let me give you a lowdown on my UK visit,' began Naveen as his minions, Arpita and Usha, grinned from ear to ear in approval. (Arpita's smile was definitely fake but Usha's seemed real.) 'Usha, please let's have the slides.'

As if on cue, Usha took charge of the OHP (overhead projector) that began to throw images of PowerPoint presentations, weird histograms and pie charts, photographs and the like, on the white screen in front.

It was like showing coded computer programmes to crows. Hardly anything made sense but most of the 'crows' managed to carry the highly phony 'oh-that's-so-interesting' look on their faces.

'...Next. Yes. That's again me, with the CEO of Majyqri, Ms Shirley Ryder...she is the reason you all have a job. She writes your cheques, decides your salary, and is your annadaata...and let me tell you, Shirley is not happy with your performance...

'I had personally promised her sales of 1,000 units per week. You guys sold only 500 units last week! That's like marrying a woman and making her deliver half a baby!

'Someone is fucking up majorly and I want answers! You aren't some process virgins—you are expected to be as sales-savvy as seasoned whores!

'I want all of you to come forward and tell me what the hell is going on!' thundered Naveen.

The 'below-par' performers were made to squeak sheepishly as Naveen grilled them.

A few girls sniffled and a few guys turned crimson.

The 'above-average' performers (Jana and I, and three others) were not even congratulated—instead, we were given irksome dope like 'don't be complacent', 'raise the bar', etc.

Arpita and Usha weren't spared either.

'If you recruit dodos, you can't expect them to fly like eagles. Perform or perish! From next week, we will have new floor-walkers who will also double up as practice coaches.

'Come on, even the local sabzi-wallah knows how to sell. Pity the city's vegetable vendors don't know English, otherwise they would do better than most of you guys. That's all for now. Dismissed!' screamed Naveen.

We moved out, either sullen or angry.

Some of the girls were in tears. But for the protective steel railing hemming in the terrace, they would have gladly taken the plunge into the sprawling expanse of the Durga temple below. It would have been nice to see Naveen 'Kutta' Katyal being charged with abetment to mass suicide, but life seldom converts your wishes into reality.

'I think the Majyqri guys collectively sodomized him at a group orgy,' said Roshan, the fourth-best in our team.

'Yeah, no wonder this guy has begun farting from his mouth ever since. His rear is all jammed up,' said Shubra, the cattiest of our lot, and we all laughed hysterically.

꒰

An hour later, Jana and I were summoned to Naveen's cabin—minimalist but elegant. An Anjolie Ela Menon painting adorned the right wall. The left wall just carried a whiteboard with the names of our principal clients, the team leads handling them, plus the top performers sitting below two arrows.

That was us! Our names adorned the boss's wall!

I beamed mentally and my chest swelled enough to compete with Pamela Anderson.

As we entered he just gestured, asking us to sink into the plush leather chairs, while his eyes continued to bore into his laptop screen.

'Shit!' he said, and I scribbled in the writing pad we were always supposed to carry for important meetings:

'Is that an exclamation or an order? Will he also provide the toilet paper?'

Jana smothered his chuckle by covering his mouth.

'Vishy, that was an exclamation, not an order,' Naveen said after two minutes, and we both looked amazed.

'I am sorry, Sir?' I said, pretending infantile innocence. 'I didn't get you.'

'Cut the crap. No "sir" here or anywhere else, just call me Naveen...and fuck the lies...look up,' he said.

We both looked at the ceiling. What was that tiny red glow? The small recess in the false ceiling definitely held something. A hidden camera?

'That's a high resolution gizmo, one of the latest. I can see what you shared with Jana just now on my laptop. I am the eye in the sky, wotsay?' he laughed.

'I...I...am sorry...Sir...Naveen, I was just kidding...' I stammered.

'Forget it...good comment. I like people with a sense of humour. They make the best salesmen. Okay, let me swing into action. I have called you guys here because you are the best telecallers in the Majyqri process.'

'Thank you, Naveen!' I beamed.

'Welcome. Congrats and all that crap! In one month, you have done wonders! As usual, Usha's team has outscored Arpita's...'

I blanched as he said 'Usha.' Did he sigh ever so slightly when he took her name, or was I just imagining it? Were they really seeing each other, or was it one of those unfounded corporate rumours regarding office romance?

'So now you both have to wear an extra hat each,' he continued.

'Like?' I asked, clearly alarmed. (In corporate circles 'extra hat' meant 'we are going to treat you like a donkey fit to carry more workload.')

A zillion thoughts criss-crossed my biocomputer.

Would he ask us to do overtime? Would he make us join Arpita's team? Damn, wouldn't I get to ogle Usha perched so seductively at her console? Would I never get congratulatory hugs from her again?

'Relax,' said Naveen to me. 'You look as if I'm about to ask you to volunteer for the guillotine! It's nothing as medieval or dramatic. It's good news. I want both of you to double up as trainee floor-walkers!'

'Wow!' I exclaimed. 'Really?'

'Of course, the client wants us to use our present resources. Cost-cutting and all that shit. So congrats on your promotion...'

'Oh, that's wonderful! Thanks a million, Naveen,' I gasped.

Jana was deep in thought. His eyes were focused on a distant time zone. Had Nostradamus carried a similar expression when he had penned (or quilled) his quatrains?

'Out with it, Jana. Keeping corporate secrets is a non-bailable offence in this room,' said Naveen, smiling.

'Well, you know, it could create some bad blood in the team...' said Jana.

'Oh, damn all that!' said Naveen, with a dismissive wave of his hand. 'Of course people will be envious... A piece of advice: go ahead and bitch about me, say that I am an *asshole* who asked you guys to help a few others do better... that always works.

'And remember, guys...have them selling, please...my ass is on fire here, and you are my fire extinguishers, okay?'

'Sure, Naveen, you can bank on us...' I said eagerly.

'Buzz off now and send in Usha. Yeah, and Arpita too,' said Naveen, shooing us away.

'Vishy, I don't like the overall feeling on this one,' whispered Jana as we exited the boss's lair.

'C'mon yaar, stop being so cynical!' I said. 'This is a wonderful break for both of us and we can move up the corporate ladder in a jiffy. Don't spoil the sweet taste of victory crystallizing in my mouth...'

'Some victories are Pyrrhic,' he observed.

'What hic?'

'Pyrrhic—means a victory gained at a great cost,' he explained, shaking his head.

'What a cynic you are, Jana! Always trying to look for a dark cloud around any silver lining! If someone gifted you the Kohinoor, you'd suspect they are out to sabotage your genius with some diamond-generated radiation poisoning!' I remarked.

Jana continued to shake his head as we headed towards the floor.

'Bitch about the boss, act sad and morose, exactly what the boss ordered...' I kept chanting all along the way.

'Hey, guys, what transpired between you and the big boss?' asked Usha as we sat down at our consoles.

'That bloody pompous asshole wants us to do some extra work,' I screamed, ensuring that everyone got the message.

'Language, please! Have some respect for your superiors,' rebuked Usha.

The entire team smiled at me and I knew that I had won them over. Machiavellian corporate politics at its best. I was the Call Centre Chanakya.

'By the way, the *respectable* bastard wants your *respectful* presence in his cabin, right away,' I said to Usha, and the floor guffawed.

'You are incorrigible!' said Usha. 'If he overhears all this, even I won't be able to save your ass.'

If only she knew, I thought.

'No probs, my ass is boss-proof anyway. And yeah, take Arpita along with you.'

ᔛ

After the official announcement had been made, I was quite surprised to note that almost nobody seemed to be envious. Either they all were great actors or genuinely happy for us.

'So guys,' said Usha to the cafeteria crowd, 'give a warm welcome to your new floor-walkers.'

Everyone screamed and hurrahed and began the congratulatory routine.

'Okay, enough of the clichés, now Jana and Vishy will chalk out their game plan with all of you—teams, take this as an impromptu brainstorming session,' ordered Arpita.

'What game plan?' I asked.

'Oho, stop pretending to be dumb,' said Usha.

'Yeah, don't behave like a work-shirker,' said Arpita.

'Okay, we'll evolve some methodology to enhance sales and make your boss happy,' smiled Jana.

The next half hour saw us discussing call flow stats, customer behavioural pattern, demographic analysis and 'demotivating Katyal kutta's' speech.

I increased my fan base by launching a tirade against Naveen that included lots of 'maa-kis' and 'behen-kis' in it, and much else besides. At the end of the day, we did the good employee thing of designing some PowerPoint presentations and Excel sheets to impress Naveen.

Jana had the minor job of thinking up innovative ideas, while I did the major part of keying in the stuff he dictated. C'mon, stop sniggering! Thinking is so easy and typing so very difficult.

The Secret of My Success

Fortune favours the restless mind.

Two months into my new role and the drab coach-counsel-call routine was enough to make me feel cloistered. I was raring to do something new. The good part was that my vocabulary had improved phenomenally. But I was clearly bored. How long can you teach people to sell phones, and convince yourself that life is fun?

I used to sit for hours at the Burning Ghat, pondering my situation. For some strange reason, Jana never frequented the ghat now—perhaps he wanted to bury the memories of the past? I didn't ask. There were other important queries to be dealt with.

Surely there was more to life than this? Isn't contentment an escape route for those who don't like to push themselves? Shouldn't one try to get more from life, rather than try to preserve what one already has? Isn't conquering newer peaks the very stuff that life's made up of?

The ABC juice at Buddha Bakery didn't taste as good as usual. The attractive women didn't seem as alluring as earlier. The chatter wasn't as disturbing as before. I had slipped into some kind of insulated drabness; no, it wasn't depression or something, just plain boredom, as if I were stuck in a rut. I felt like a garage-confined, cruelly-grounded, frustrated Ferrari. I longed to exit the corporate comfort zone and zoom ahead.

Everything seemed so dull that I could have seen rainbows in black and white. Life was passing me by and I gazed longingly at all those who seemed to have made it in life: the guys who came in Pajeros, the rich sanyasi sporting a jazzy Rolex watch, the spoilt brat who came in an Alfa Romeo, the lady wedded to a Louis Vuitton handbag—and I suddenly wanted it all.

How could I get more success, and be more confident and happy? What else could I do? Balls to Majyqri and Cosmos, they wouldn't create my future. *I will create my future.* How to become rich and famous? The vortex of unbridled ambition pulled me in and kept me submerged for a long while... I visualized myself in a success story, where I, the hero, would finally get all that he desired.

'Hello,' said a voice as someone plonked himself next to me.

'Hi,' I said, and saw that he wasn't alone. The uber-funky girl about to sit opposite me seemed familiar. Where had I seen her before? I couldn't quite place her.

'You stay here? I mean in Pune?' he asked.

'Yeah,' I said laconically, as I was in no mood for casual conversation.

'I am Harry Kashyap, and this is Nimika Chandok, we are from Mumbai,' he explained.

'Welcome to Pune,' I said tiredly.

'Thanks. By the way, I had seen you last month, too. We keep driving down,' Harry explained. 'Actually, we are ad film-makers, surely you must have seen Nimika in the recent Paris Pari soap commercial. I made that.'

Oh yeah, so that's why she looked familiar. Not that I watched much TV—her image must have gotten implanted subliminally as I grabbed a few snippets of some cricket match.

'Yeah, I guess I have,' I said to her, 'though I find real life more interesting than TV. No offence meant.'

'None taken,' smiled Nimika.

'Sorry, I haven't even asked you your name,' said Harry.

'Vishy.'

'Well, Vishy, I will come straight to the point. Actually I am planning to make a low-budget movie, a corporate comedy of sorts, set in an ad agency, about how a political party refuses to pay the dues after they lose the elections, and how the hero and heroine get the money from them—a bit like Jeffrey Archer's *Not a Penny Less, Not a Penny More* kind of thing.'

I wondered why he was telling me all this.

'Seems to be a nice idea,' I said.

'It is; the script has shaped up rather well,' said Nimika.

'Yeah, it's cool, and we auditioned quite a few people in Mumbai. Actually, the guys we like are demanding too much and the guys who are willing to do it we don't like. Typical casting quandary,' said Harry.

So? What's all that got to do with me? Am I some kind of Agony Uncle you pour your troubles out to on a Sunday evening? Buzz off, you jokers, don't tell me your troubles, I have troubles of my own, I thought.

'We need a new face. Would you be interested?' asked Nimika.

'Yeah, you got the physique and the looks, can you act?' asked Harry.

'*What!*' I exclaimed, thoroughly dumbfounded.

'Can you act?' Harry repeated. 'You know, drama and stuff like that?'

'You mean, you want me to be an actor in your movie?' I asked.

'Arre, not just an actor, the main lead,' said Nimika.

'Wow! Are you guys serious, or is this some kind of belated April Fool joke?' I wondered aloud.

'We are dead serious. Nimika is the female lead. Wait, let me show you the script,' he said, and fished out a spiral-bound script titled *Paisa To Gul Total Cool* from his bag.

I flipped through the A-4-size papers and couldn't believe my luck! Just when I was wondering how to scale new summits in life, life had chosen to pour down a windfall! Me? An actor? Why not? Could I pull it off? Of course! Whether you think you can or you can't, you are right—not my line—methinks that's by Henry Ford.

I was magically transported to the future in an instant... I smiled at the paparazzi while posing for umpteen photo-ops. I delivered a fundu speech that had everyone in splits as I collected my first best actor award. I denied having an affair with Catherine Zeta-Jones after Steven Spielberg cast us together...

'Any place where we can do a screen test?' asked Harry, breaking my daydream.

'Huh? Sure, we can go to my pad, it's close by...' I said.

'Great, actually our hotel is far off, in Shivaji Nagar, or we could have gone there. I have a handycam, so Nimika and you can do a scene or two...I can show it to my partner, too, and we can take a call later...cool?'

'Yeah, super-cool,' I said, and we began heading for Famous Heights II. Was the name of our apartment a kind of divine signal that I was going to scale exactly that in the near future?

༄

Thankfully, Jana and Arpita had gone for the White Lotus Chakra Healing evening meeting at the commune, so I wouldn't feel too conscious auditioning for this godsend.

I pulled out two Budweiser cans from the refrigerator to seem hospitable. We settled down in the living room.

'Oh, thanks,' said Nimika as I placed the stuff on the glass-topped cane table. 'Harry, why don't you tell us which scene you'd like us to enact?'

'I guess Bawa would like the sitting-on-the-lap scene to begin with,' he told her, and turning to me, 'Bawa is our partner and fellow producer. I will be directing the movie, of course.'

'Cool,' I said. 'How do we go about it?'

'I will run you through the scene. You are Jeet and she is Meena in the movie,' said Harry.

'Okay,' I said.

'I want you to imagine yourself as a successful, brash, arrogant upstart—someone who's a self-made man. You are a confident, totally sure of yourself, super-intelligent kind of guy. Got it?'

'Yeah, that's me, no doubt. You just described my personality profile, Harry,' I said, and they both laughed as they sipped the beer.

'And the scene is romantic plus slightly erotic—I am a senior client servicing executive you recruited a year ago,' explained Nimika. 'Initially, we don't like each other too much, but after the political party cheats us, I agree to help you get back the money. This is when our romance develops. In this scene, we are in your office cabin, and I am sitting on your lap, and you have to slowly run your hands along my back, and as we say the dialogues, slowly you have to squeeze the side of my butt...'

Man, this was fun! A hot chick on my lap was definitely what I needed! And I also get to paw her? Amazing! Bollywood zindabad, low budget, high budget, whatever! The lustometer would now have said: Nimika>Usha>Shalini>Arpita.

'Hmmm...okay...and dialogues?' I said nonchalantly, careful not to sound too eager about the erotic bit.

'I am coming to that,' said Harry, extending the spiral-bound script. 'Here, go through pages 15 and 16...'

We went through the dialogues and both of them guided me on the intonation, emphasis, pauses and stuff. Nimika was definitely a natural.

They said I was okay with the dialogues, but my expressions needed to be more subtle.

'Be real, as if she is really your girlfriend, *feel it*,' said

Harry, and I closed my eyes for a few seconds, imagining Nimika to be Usha.

We rehearsed our parts for about ten minutes (no, without her warming my lap) and Harry asked me if I was ready.

'Okay, forget I am here, dissolve into your character, melt into it, she is Meena, she is Meena; forget you are Vishy, you are Jeet, you are Jeet, action!' he shouted, steadying the handycam.

Nimika moved towards the sofa, and I kept mentally chanting 'don't get a hard-on and embarrass yourself, Jeet', as I thought of Rajesh Khanna to get the right expression of romance on my face.

She moved seductively, coolly placed herself on my lap, and I somehow succeeded in preventing my groin from reacting.

We cootchie-cooed for some five minutes, saying our lines softly...

I ran my hand along her back, wondering if I should squeeze her butt passionately or lovingly, and settled for somewhere in between.

Just as Harry said 'cut' the door flew open.

Darn! Arpita and Jana had let themselves in with the spare key! Arpita's face registered everything from pure horror to controlled anger within the space of a few nanoseconds. Jana seemed cool, as if he was used to seeing a hot chick on my lap every other day.

'What the hell!' said Arpita. 'Are we interrupting a homemade soft porn session?'

'Oh, hi! Arpi...Arpi...actually...' I stuttered as Nimika effortlessly slid off my lap and into the sofa. 'Hey, meet

Harry, and this is Nimika. Guys, this is Arpita, and that's my best buddy, Jana...we share this pad...'

'Will someone explain what the hell's going on here?' screamed Arpita, and Harry came to my rescue.

'Please, don't be so shocked. I am a film-maker from Mumbai, we bumped into Vishy at Buddha Bakery, and I am screen-testing him for a role in my debut Hindi movie...' said Harry.

'*Movie?* Since when, Vishy? Is this really happening or am I trapped in some dream?' exclaimed Arpita.

'Harry, show her the script,' suggested Nimika, pointing towards the glass-topped cane table, and Jana picked it up.

'Aha, nice title, Arpi. Take a look. *Paisa To Gul Total Cool,*' said Jana, 'and meet Vishy, the new King Con.'

'Yeah, Arpi, c'mon, we could have gone to their hotel but it is far off...so I thought...' I said.

'Fine,' said Arpita laconically as she made for her room. 'No explanations needed. Whatever. It's your place too. Okay guys, bye, I'm kind of tired.'

Harry and Nimika got ready to leave and I apologized for Arpita's bluntness. Jana, too, chipped in by adding, 'She's just had a bad day, don't mind it guys, plus she's very possessive about Vishy, hope you find him suitable for the role, he's a born actor and all.'

'No probs,' said Harry smilingly. 'I have taken much worse in my career. I understand. Must have been a shock, seeing him cosying up with Nimika like that—'

'Yeah, we are cool. Vishy, keep in touch,' said Nimika, thrusting a business card into my hand that said: 'Train Ticket Films. Partners: Harry Kashyap, Bawa Mirchandani,

Nimika Chandok'. 'Look us up when you come to Mumbai next.'

We saw them off at the gates. Nimika stored my mobile number in her cell and gave me a missed call. I saw them laughing animatedly as they walked away.

They were probably discussing Arpita's horrified expression and later boorish behaviour.

I was so livid that I didn't feel like talking to Arpita. I decided to go to the ghat to extinguish the fires of indignation—how dare she react like that, as if I was some kind of sex maniac? And I had long been under the impression that she was a modern, broad-minded, bindaas girl! How wrong I had been! Her mental bandwidth was so narrow!

Jana offered to cool Arpita down by explaining that this was indeed a miraculous, thoroughly unexpected break for me, and sauntered back to our pad. Actually, I was the one who needed to be cooled down by his soothing presence, but we couldn't clone Jana, could we? So I let him handle the hyperventilating woman instead.

ॐ

There is something about the Burning Ghat that evaporates your immediate thoughts. Perhaps it is the tranquil peepul trees lining it, or the majestic finality of life that it symbolizes, or the ultimate realization that life is just an irritant in transit, or the sanyasis staying there who seem not to have a care in the world—something (or everything) about the ghat is designed to throw your EEG patterns into neutral gear and events into perspective.

I rebuked myself for having staged a walkout like some disgruntled parliamentarian. Shouldn't I have been more understanding and taken a mature view of things? Perhaps I would have reacted the same way if I had seen Arpita in someone's lap, with a Sony handycam filming the prurient goings-on.

Anyway, what was done was done. As a gentle breeze rustled through the trees and sang its soft lullaby, I just dozed off. After what must have been an hour or so, I felt someone trying to shake me awake. But I was still floating in the comforting calm of an oceanic reverie. Life is so much more fun when you are fast asleep, isn't it?

'Hey boy! Wakey wakey, life is calling!' said a voice in my dream.

'What for? Is life selling something?' I mumbled.

'Yeah, buy a burger, get two friends free!' said the voice.

'Burgers are fun...but the same can't be said about friends...' I muttered.

Arpita finally punched me so hard that I woke up with a start. As I rubbed my eyes she put her arm around me, and gently ran her fingers through my hair.

'Sorry,' she said.

'Cool,' I replied. 'But couldn't you have been a little more sensitive about it? I thought you were such a liberal and liberated person—'

'I guess I am a bit possessive about you...and slightly conservative and all that...' she said.

'Hey, Vishy, don't rub it in, okay? We both were shocked,' said Jana.

'Don't lie to support her. You didn't seem taken aback at all,' I rebuked.

'Guess I am good at hiding my emotions,' said Jana.

'Anyway, forget it. Hey, tell us about it! Movie star and all, huhn? How did you meet them?' asked Arpita, ruffling my hair.

'Well,' I smiled superciliously, 'when God gives, he tears roof and gives.'

'You have already become filmy—mangling Hindi proverbs and all,' said Jana.

'Hey, but will you leave us?' asked Arpita dejectedly.

'Arre, it was just some impromptu screen test, don't read too much into it, there must be hundreds of guys auditioning for the part,' I dismissed.

'Humility doesn't suit you at all,' said Jana. 'You already have a confident smirk on your face—that's the beginning of stardom.'

'Thanks for your astute observation, Jana,' I said. 'But keep all this totally under wraps, guys, till something gets finalized. There's many a slip betwixt the cup and the lip. I don't want to be the laughing stock at Cosmos.'

'Yeah, yeah, that goes without saying, buddy,' said Arpita.

They teased me a bit about my ambitions and all—how I would eventually change into a fashion-conscious monster who would forget all his old friends in his mad race to achieve celluloid greatness and how they would only get to interact with me through Page 3 news and film magazines.

Anyway, I was finally all cheered up and ready to see rainbows in their trademark seven colours again. Hope is like opium for an ambitious mind. There's no greater high than visualizing a magnificent future for yourself. My spirit was soaring, and the high-altitude flying reminded me of Mom's words: *You will make it real big one day.*

LEVEL 10

Provoked

Hell hath no fury like a man scorned.

I think it was roughly a fortnight after my screen test—yeah, now I remember, it was a Tuesday—when I went to meet Usha at her place. (Monday was my day off that week, so I hadn't checked in at Cosmos.)

Arpita told me that Usha had reported sick on Monday, and I had this nagging feeling throughout the Tuesday shift that something was terribly wrong, as Usha had also switched off her cell. My sense of premonition was spinning horrendous images in my mind.

I did a bit of coaching, counselling and telecalling, but my heart wasn't into it. Finally, unable to contain my concern, I requested Jana to handle my team too, and sought Arpita's permission to head back home at roughly 8.30 p.m.

Only, I didn't head back to Goratown Park. I borrowed someone's bike to reach Usha's pad at Aundh, promising him that I'd be back before his shift ended.

I rode like the wind.

I rang the bell and waited for close to five minutes before Usha opened the door. What I saw was a nightmare: swollen eyes, a small bruise along the right temple, unkempt hair flying all over and a sullen expression usually carried either by those extremely hurt or totally angry—or sometimes both.

'Hi, what the hell!' I said. 'What happened?'

'Hi,' she said weakly. 'What are you doing here?'

'Came to look you up, wasn't feeling good without you around,' I said. 'Can I come in?'

'Hmm? Okay,' she said hesitantly, making sure the door stayed ajar. (I hadn't thought too much of the ajar-door thing then, but after ten minutes, I understood why.)

'Hey,' I asked, 'have you seen a doc?'

'Why? I haven't been raped!' she shouted.

Her extreme response to a totally innocuous question set me thinking. Something had definitely gone devastatingly wrong!

'Usha, please, tell me what happened?' I probed further.

'That bastard, that bastard...' she said, shaking her head, and went silent, like an assault victim. I was reminded of Rekha's menacing eyes in *Khoon Bhari Maang*.

'Who? Who are you talking about?' I asked.

'That creep, that creep...' she hissed.

'What the hell! Who did this to you?' I asked, pointing at her temple.

She just shook her head and tried to stifle her agitation.

'Usha, this is serious,' I said, moving closer to her and placing a comforting hand on her shoulder.

'Don't you dare touch me!' she screamed.

'Sorry,' I said, inching away from her, 'but at least tell me what exactly happened.'

After much coaxing, she gave me the gory details and broke down.

I was livid but didn't know what to do. Finally, I decided to go back to Cosmos (I had to return the bike anyway). But more importantly, I *had* to tell Jana and Arpita about this.

༈

On Tuesday night, after the shift had ended and everyone else had left, we huddled together in the conference room—the four of us, that is, Naveen, Arpita, Jana and me.

'Naveen,' I began, 'this is just not done. You are a bloody barbarian.'

'How dare you?' he screamed. 'I can have you fired right now for insubordination!'

'Balls,' I said. 'Consider I have resigned this minute. And Arpita, Usha and Jana resign, too.'

'What? What nonsense are you talking?' asked Naveen, uncomfortable that he wasn't in his usual domineering position in the wake of this mass mutiny.

'Yeah, Naveen, how could you?' asked Arpita.

'How could I *what*? You guys said you wanted to talk about some process glitch! What the hell is all this?' asked Naveen agitatedly.

'Sexual harassment *is* a process glitch,' said Jana coolly.

'*Sexual what*? Are you guys out of your mind?' Naveen was trying the offence-is-the-best-defence kind of thing. How pathetic! His eyes expressed fear but his tone conveyed the exact opposite.

'Look, Naveen, drop the bossy attitude and stop acting so innocent. You are a bloody prick and you know it!' screamed Arpita.

'Guys...guys...surely there's been some misunder-standing, some miscommunication...what...what's going on, buddies?' asked Naveen, piping down and clearly trying to find a way out since he knew what was coming. Only, there was no way out of this mess, not for him.

'Misunderstanding, huh? Then let's hear this,' I said, switching on Usha's dictaphone, which she used in her training sessions. 'She managed to record this on Sunday night when you had made it to her pad in your drunken stupor. I am sure the voices will seem quite familiar, you creep!'

Naveen's face became darker by the second as the dictaphone shed light on his recent misdeeds.

NAVEEN: Listen, you bitch, I have...have invested time and money in you. It's time you returned the favour. (SFX 1: Tight slap. Usha dishing out what was long overdue. Oh, sorry, forgot to tell you, SFX stands for sound effects. SFX 2: Door being shut loudly and bolted. Naveen preventing any escape route.)

USHA: You bastard! Get out this minute!

NAVEEN: Easy, girl, we have been seeing each other for some time now...a little resistance is understandable, actually, good fun...sex is just the physical manifestation of a soulful expression...

USHA: Balls! I am not seeing you! We just went for a few movies and dinners!

NAVEEN: That's the exact definition of seeing each other, my dear...

USHA: You idiot, you are drunk. Get lost before I lose my mind and do something drastic—

NAVEEN: Drastic? You threatening me? Listen, I can make you a manager in return for this small favour...that idiot Arpita, she's too frigid to make it... Not that I haven't tried with her...

(SFX 3: Glass vase shattering, Usha flinging it in self-defence.)

NAVEEN: You, you...bloody bitch...

(SFX 4: Aaaarrgghhh! Naveen grabbing her and pushing her on the living room sofa. Her right temple hitting the armrest.)

USHA: You...you animal! (SFX 5: Aaarrggghhhh! Usha kicking him between his legs. Usha's hurried footsteps rushing to the door. Usha unbolting the door and stepping outside.)

NAVEEN: Ice maiden huh? That can be fun, too...

USHA: You get out or I call the watchman right now.

NAVEEN: Yeah? You will regret this.

USHA: Buzz off!

NAVEEN: I'll leave now...but remember this doesn't end here...and don't dare breathe a word of this to anyone at Cosmos or you can kiss your tight workaholic ass goodbye!

Jana couldn't take it anymore and made the first move. He socked Naveen so hard on the jaw that Naveen's head crashed against the whiteboard behind, and his chair keeled over. Naveen fell off the chair and I clutched him by his collar, pinning him down with my right knee on his chest.

'Guys, please, no violence!' screamed Arpita.

'Shut up, Arpi, our TL nearly got raped!' said Jana. 'Just imagine, what if this had happened to you?'

'You bastard,' I said to Naveen. 'You have left Usha feeling so low and shattered!'

'Guys, please, let me make amends. I was just...just plain drunk...' Naveen lamely defended himself.

'Being drunk is no excuse,' said Jana.

'Okay, what do you guys want?' asked Naveen.

'First, you apologize to Usha,' I said, dialling my number. (I had switched phones with her.) 'Hi Usha, Naveen just got the treatment. He wishes to fall at your feet and beg for forgiveness.'

'Hello...Usha, listen...I am extremely sorry, I was drunk. Let us put all this behind us...and...and work as a team...aargghhh ...' Naveen was unable to complete his apology as Jana kicked him in his stomach and I yanked the phone.

'Work as a team, huh?' asked Jana. 'Who do you think she is? Some kind of pushover?'

'It's all over, the nightmare's over, Usha,' I said. 'Now you have two personal bodyguards...never knew Jana could come in so handy!'

'Vishy,' said Usha, sniffling slightly. 'Thanks for everything. And thank Jana, too.'

'Hey, c'mon, we are just proving our corporate sense of loyalty to our TL. Anyway, we three are coming over in a while. Keep some hot coffee ready for us, okay?' I said.

'Cool,' said Usha. 'I am an insomniac in any case.'

Usha, Arpita, Jana and I did a conference call with Duniya on Wednesday. He usually managed the Indian arm of his business from the UK, and flew down to India occasionally, perhaps once every three months. Arpita had made a digital copy of the Usha–Naveen recording and patched it through to him the night before.

'Good morning, Deepak,' said Arpita. 'Sorry for the bother but we are all a bit stunned, though Usha has recovered from the shock. Now, please speak to her...'

'Hi, people!' said Duniya. 'I'm extremely sorry about all this. Naveen has been fired. And Usha? You okay? I hope you aren't pressing charges. It will be bad for our corporate image. Please accept my apologies...'

'Yeah, Deepak, I'm okay... No, I'm not pressing charges, I don't wish to have my name dragged into this mess any further, let's move on,' said Usha.

'Great, that's the spirit... Hmmm...this has definitely created a vacancy...one of you will have to stand in for Naveen... Arpi, you will be the ops manager...and Usha, you will be at the same level, as the training manager... You guys can trade places every now and then and directly report to me. Of course, you both get a hike of ₹18,000. Are we all cool about this?' said Duniya.

'Super!' they chorused.

'Okay, Jana, you take over from Arpi as TL. This is a pucca position. A seven-grand raise; ditto for Vishy, you can handle Usha's team, okay?' said Duniya.

'Done, boss.'

'Okay, if there's nothing else, I gotta go now. Congratulations on your new roles! See you guys soon!' he said.

'Bye, Deepak, take care,' we chorused.
'Rock the scene folks, bye!' he said.

ॐ

We four were chilling out at Usha's pad one Thursday night, after our shift ended, as Friday was a national holiday in the UK, and by extension, a holiday for us too. The three of them were guzzling beer and I had mixed some chaat masala in my Coke to make it tangier. Usha was looking lovely in her fluffy pink top and long white skirt. Alanis Morissette was singing in the background, while Jana was saying that he wanted to listen to some Led Zep or Jethro Tull. We all hooted him down for being so very ancient in his choice of bands.

'Let's dance and celebrate our newfound success,' said Usha, pulling me off the sofa, and turning to Jana, 'You are next, partner, get ready for some terpsichorean torture after I am done with your friend with the two left feet here...'

'What's terpsi ...whatever...Korean?' I asked.

'Arre, idiot, you don't know simple English or what? Terpsichorean means "of or related to dancing" just like asinine refers to an ass like you...she's just ragging you...' mocked Jana.

'Yeah, yeah, rag them hard, Usha, they are both our bloody juniors,' said Arpita, sniggering loudly. 'You both are our slaves...if we want you to do a striptease routine, you will have to do it pronto...'

'Well, that comes under the purview of sexual harassment, Mizz Arpita Katyal,' said Jana, and we all laughed.

'Guys, please don't remind me of that creep,' pleaded Usha.

'Okay, relax... Hey Arpi, let's play strip poker,' said Jana.

'Don't you have a mother–sister at home?' asked Arpita.

'They haven't graduated beyond snakes and ladders,' he retorted.

'You guys are all drunk and talking shit,' I said.

'Stop jiving like a pansy, Vishy,' said Jana. 'Save it for the bloody movies you will eventually do... Hey, Usha, this fellow is going to be a movie star...a hot babe was sitting on his lap the other day...and...Arpi, tell her, na, about it...'

Jana began laughing hysterically and I could have strangled him for his catty comment, but I was enjoying the dance, with my arm around Usha's waist, so I let it pass.

'Shut up, Jana! Stop teasing him about *that*!' said Arpita.

'What's he laughing about? What babe?' asked Usha.

'Arre, somebody wanted me to take a screen test and all. Some low-budget movie...Mumbai ad film-maker...and these two barged in while we were filming a romantic scene and behaved as if we were shooting for some blue film, the bloody perverts—' I explained.

'Cool,' said Usha, 'you have the personality to be a film star, you know?'

'You think so?' I said.

'I know so,' said Usha, and her compliment made me so happy that I felt like hugging and kissing her.

'Hey, Usha,' said Arpita. 'Since we are no longer corporate rivals, why don't you stay with us? It will be fun, all of us together. Also, Vishy might be leaving in a while.'

'Stay at your pad, you mean?' asked Usha.

'Yeah, wow, Arpi! You come up with swell ideas!' I said.

'Nah, what will I do with this place?' wondered Usha.

'Arre, we will use this place as our hideout. Escape zone,' said Jana. 'C'mon, we'll have loads of masti there. What Aundh? GP is the happening spot. Plus, a lovely girl like you shouldn't stay alone.'

'Yeah, Usha,' I said. 'Don't worry, we are safe people. Jana is impotent and I am so well-mannered—'

'Vishy, you know what's the difference between seduction and rape?' asked Jana.

'What?' I asked.

'Salesmanship,' he said, and the girls burst into uncontrollable peals of laughter. (Ethyl alcohol makes even PJs seem funny.)

'Okay, Usha, you game?' asked Arpita.

'It's an idea,' said Usha.

'Great! Then we will shift your stuff in the morning,' I said.

Fools Rush In

Do things your way, or not at all.

The four of us lived like split personalities and it was kind of fun. We never brought happenings at the workplace back home. It was as if our behavioural patterns changed with our geographical position.

At Sepoy Gokhale Road, we were pucca professionals, not giving in an inch, not letting our friendship cloud our ergonomic judgements. The lines were clearly drawn, and both Usha and Arpita graded us ruthlessly on the performance appraisal reports that reached Duniya with religious regularity every fortnight.

Jana usually scored a zero in 'compliance with best practices'—thanks to his fiercely independent spirit—and a stratospherically high grade in nearly everything else.

I did well too, but was always second best, though I had got used to that by now.

At Goratown Park, we were like langotiya yaars, totally inseparable, fabulously cheerful and completely at ease with each other's eccentricities and weaknesses.

Nearly two months had passed after that screen test and I had given up all hope of becoming an 'actor-shactor' as Jana kept saying. In fact, now that Usha was staying with us, I didn't feel like quitting Cosmos at all.

Usha and I became really close during those days—I mean intellectually and emotionally, not physically, you dirty minds. Life no longer seemed drab, and I didn't want to break free from the routine. It suited me just fine actually.

It's funny what a loved one's presence can do to your earlier sense of ennui and angst against getting stuck in a ruthless rut. Now, the rut seemed divine, joyous, blissful and positively soul elevating.

I would help Usha dry her hair, hang out her stuff on the clothesline, make bed-tea for her, keep a rose or a carnation next to her bed, never say that I loved her, never expect her to say it either—and it became apparent to us that the language of true romance was silence mixed with the occasional twinkle in the eye.

We would go to Taozen Teerth Park in the mornings, admire the lush surrounds and the birdsong, grab an early breakfast at Buddha Bakery, read the newspapers and try to outdo each other on the crossword section, come back to our pad, watch TV, listen to music, play Scrabble, whistle up lunch together, grab a quick post-prandial siesta, wake each other up for our 4.30 p.m. shift and get dressed hurriedly. If we missed the cab, we were happy about it because we could then zoom along on Usha's Kinetic Honda, and she would hold me tight and make me feel on top of the world.

Jana and Arpita were equally inseparable, but theirs was more the platonic version of togetherness, though we never openly discussed our nascent romance with either of them. I wasn't a religious person or anything, in fact I was a bit of an atheist—I still am—but I definitely remember having prayed on many nights that our cosy status quo should continue forever.

Love Story

What's sweet to begin with becomes bitter eventually.

That cosy status quo lasted some forty-five days. One Sunday, I got a call from Nimika. I didn't know whether to feel happy or sad after the call. Perhaps my heart amalgamated a bit of both emotions.

Usha had been in the shower when the call came. I struggled till 5 p.m. to break the news to her. Arpita and Jana had gone to the Taozen commune in the wee hours and they would spend the entire day there, so I thought there would be no one to console Usha when she heard about my plans.

'Sorry, couldn't call you up earlier since we were still scouting for the male lead. My condolences, Vishy, I have bad news for you,' Nimika had said.

'Yeah, cool,' I'd said. 'I knew I hadn't made it.'

'Wrong,' she'd laughed. 'When I said "bad news" I meant you are going to become a superstar...too bad that you will be mobbed everywhere and you can never again have a moment of peace in your life—unless you migrate to Mongolia or something...'

'Pardon?' I'd said excitedly. 'You mean...you mean...'

'Yup, buddy! You are the main lead now. Harry and I are driving down this evening. We will be at the Orchid Hotel at Shivaji Nagar. Try to meet us at 7 p.m. We'll discuss your signing amount, the contract and all. Bawa might also accompany us or join us later, let's see...'

'Wow! You serious?'

'Absolutely, and when we do the actual shoot, pinch my butt harder, you were too gentlemanly during the screen test; the public wants hardcore stuff, buddy. Ciao, then... catch you in the evening!'

'Thanks, Nimika! This is wonderful! And give my thanks to Harry and Bawa, too!'

'I will. Take care, Vishy, bye.'

ॐ

The couple walking hand in hand at Taozen Teerth Park made me sigh. Those leading simple, unambitious lives seemed to have everything sorted. Work, earn, survive the day, romance on weekends, marry, settle down, have kids, spend a bit, save a bit and continue the monotonous cycle till some unseen force pulls you out of it all. But what's the point, I thought. Even beggars survive. To get something, one needs to lose other things. Life is a self-service cafeteria and you choose the dishes. You can't have all on your plate, so one has to go for the most exotic—

'Say something,' said Usha. 'You are reminding me of Rodin's sculpture, *The Thinker*.'

'Hmmm...I have to tell you something, Usha dear...' I hesitated.

'Tell me then. What are you holding back? You have fallen in love with someone else? No problems. *Tumse jaan chooti toh laakhon paaye*,' she laughed.

'It's much worse than that,' I said morosely.

'Hey, out with it! What's biting you?' she said.

'I will have to leave Pune and settle down in Mumbai,' I said.

'What? Why? You getting a better job?' she asked.

'Sort of. Nimika called this morning and I have to meet them in two hours. They have cast me in their movie as the lead...'

'Woohoo! That's fantastic news! We should be celebrating—why are you so glum?' she screamed, thwacking me on the shoulder. 'And why didn't you tell me earlier, you fool!'

'Huh? Here I was worrying about how you'd take it, and you seem elated!' I sounded surprised.

'Why shouldn't I be elated, you nut! This is great news! What are you worried about?' she asked.

'Us,' I said. 'What about us? I'll have to shift base now...'

'Are you mad or something? You are talking as if this is the end of us. I will also take up some job in Mumbai—what's the problem?' she said.

'You will? But you said two months ago that it's your dream to be the CEO of Cosmos, that you hate the hustle and bustle of Mumbai, that you never want to leave the laid-back serenity of Pune,' I reminded her.

'Arre, damn all that. That was all before *we* happened to each other. Equations change, Vishy. Now, I can't live without you. And since Bollywood isn't going to migrate, Usha will have to,' she smiled.

I hugged her long and hard when she said that, and wept tears of joy as she cradled me in her arms.

'Cutiepie, you were worried that I wouldn't react well to this, right?' she asked.

'Hmm,' I murmured, overwhelmed by emotions and gratitude.

'You'll make a great romantic hero, crybaby,' she said, stroking my hair.

Ah, heaven.

∾

'Hi Nimika,' I said as she opened the door to their suite at Orchid Hotel. 'Meet Usha, my girlfriend.'

'Hi Usha!' cooed Nimika, guiding us in. 'Welcome, welcome, so the handsome hunk is already ensnared? How sad!'

'I thought Sunday evenings were reserved for Buddha Bakery visits?' I said, settling into the sofa.

'Not this time, buddy, lots of things to do, actually we got what we wanted from the bakery,' said Nimika.

'And what's that?' I asked.

'You!' said Nimika, with a mischievous glint in her eyes.

'How many guys did you audition for the role?' asked Usha.

'Hey, by the way, where is Harry?' I butted in.

'He's gone down to the coffee shop, some guest he wanted to meet alone. Should be here anytime now,' said

Nimika to me, and turning to Usha, 'Hmm...well...a rough estimate would make it close to two hundred, I'd say.'

'Wow! So many?' I asked.

'Well, Vishy, there's a lot riding on this for us... Just a sec...lemme text Harry that you are here...' said Nimika, while Usha whispered to me that she'd like to take a look at my debut screen test, and I shushed her.

'What are you lovebirds so secretive about?' asked Nimika.

'Oh nothing, she wants to see the screen test,' I said.

'Aha, Harry has the CD, cool, we'll show it to you, Usha,' said Nimika. 'What would you guys like to have? Juice, coffee, burgers?'

'Nothing, thanks,' said Usha.

'Yeah, we just gorged at the bakery,' I said.

'Cool, we will have dinner together later... Vishy, here, take a look at the new script,' she said, extending a manila folder. 'That's your copy, study it well.'

'New? Major changes?' I asked.

'Not major, actually. Just tweaked a few dialogues, removed the clichés, added a few scenes, songs, etc....' said Nimika, and as she heard the knock, '...think Harry has come.'

'Hi, Vishy! Howdy, superstar!' said Harry, hugging me.

'Harry, this is Usha, my GF,' I said.

'Ah, Usha, great personality, definitely the heroine in my next—' said Harry.

'No thanks, I don't like applying greasepaint and all,' smiled Usha. 'One actor in the family is enough!'

'My loss!' said Harry cheerfully.

'Thanks, Harry, for taking me on,' I said.

'Hell, no! You were the best, and Nimika feels you are going to just rock the scene. I wish you could have met Bawa though... Well, definitely in Mumbai...'

'So he isn't coming?' asked Nimika.

'No, he's gotta meet the art director, some songwriters, etc., etc.,' said Harry. 'Okay, Vishy, now let's get down to business.'

'Sure,' I said.

'Here's the contract, read it well,' said Harry, extending a few sheets.

'I will, but later,' I said. 'Just give me the gist.'

'Spoken like a pucca pro,' said Harry. 'It's simple. You can't do another romantic comedy for a year, unless *we* make one, and you can't sign up with any other producer, either. Only for a year, though. After that, you're a free bird. We pay you a signing amount of five lakh initially. Then we pay you 2.5 after the first month of shooting. The balance 2.5 when we complete the dubbing. Total ten, bas. Cool?'

'Of course, Harry, sounds good to me,' I said.

'Great, I hope Usha doesn't mind, but I'd like you to jam with Nimika on the script. Shooting starts in exactly fifteen days. You got a place to stay in Mumbai?' asked Harry.

'No,' I said, 'but I guess we can manage something.'

'Yeah, I have a few pals there, and they can help us find some acco—' said Usha.

'Oh, you are also coming, Usha?' Harry enquired.

'Yeah, we are kind of inseparable now,' she said.

'Cool. Okay, not to worry. Nimika, ask Sharma to hook up with some agent in Lokhandwala. Get a nice 2 BHK at least. Partly furnished. With AC etc., max one week,' said Harry.

'Done, boss,' nodded Nimika.

'And what would the rent be? And deposit?' asked Usha.

'Hey, don't you worry about all that,' Harry reassured. 'I am arranging it. We will pay. You just enjoy. I am a good paymaster but I will make Vishy slog, too.'

'Very kind of you, Harry, you're an angel,' I said.

'Not at all! I am just a smart businessman who can spot potential from miles away, so I gotta use you to the max before you become a superstar and charge the kind of money that I can't afford,' smiled Harry.

'Don't say that, Harry. You will become real big too, and will be able to afford anything,' I said.

'*Tumhare mooh mein cookies aur chocolate*,' said Nimika.

'If I get cavities, my voice will echo,' I jibed.

'You guys have great chemistry,' laughed Harry.

'Hey, I forgot, Harry, Usha wants to see the screen test,' said Nimika.

'Sure,' he said. 'Wait, lemme get the CD.'

He played it for us and Usha kept giggling throughout, and then we all burst into laughter because Harry had also recorded Arpita's huffy fit!

'My! My! That woman sure was scandalized,' grinned Usha.

'You bet,' said Harry, 'she thought we were making some Penthouse home video.'

'Usha, you don't mind our intimate scenes, do you?' Nimika wanted to know.

'Of course not. Vishy knows his limits. And I trust the two of you. Today's heroes and heroines do worse stuff, so this is cool... In some films, the hero slips a spinning top into the heroine's navel and all, how vulgar can you get! You guys are at least classy,' said Usha sportingly.

'Yeah, true... Vishy, you have an understanding girlfriend,' said Nimika.

'But that's only because I haven't yet told her about the swimming pool scene,' I said.

'*Haan, glamour ke bina toh koi bhi picture nahin chalti hai these days*,' said Harry.

'Swimming pool? Nimika, or someone else?' asked Usha.

'Well, I am supposed to be in a two-piece bikini, song sequence and all. Then Vishy rubs some suntan oil on my back after undoing my bikini strap and some shit like that,' explained Nimika.

'I am cool—sounds like fun actually—but Vishy's parents are kinda conservative,' warned Usha.

'Ooh, are they?' asked Nimika.

'Arre, she's just kidding,' I lied, and defended them with an oxymoron. 'They are traditionally modern.'

'Usha, you shouldn't worry. Acting is just acting. In fact, heroes and heroines hardly develop any feelings for each other,' said Harry.

'I know, I was reading an interview of Sarwin Narang, and he said that he feels more love for his maid than for any of the hot babes,' laughed Usha.

'How very demeaning!' Nimika made a face.

We discussed the script for a while, including the characterization, costume, rehearsals, song-and-dance routines, music, a few suggestions I had, call sheets, cameras, choreography, media buzz, promos and stuff as Usha looked on, amazed. Perhaps she was wondering how I knew so much about the film industry (well, well, I had done a bit of research on the Internet, and read a few books about it too, since forewarned is forearmed, right?)

An excellent Chinese dinner later, Usha and I headed back to GP.

I was on song. The evening had breezed along like a dream on steroids. I had inked the contract after a brief, cursory look. Harry had been pleased about that. I patted the family photograph in my shirt pocket. Usha's handbag carried the contract and my first major pay cheque. Wow! ₹5 lakh! More than what I could hope to earn at Cosmos in a year. Life was good. Life was a gift. Life was a bloody godsend.

'Let's go to the bakery, we will take Arpi and Jana for a late-night cappuccino,' Usha shouted in my ear as I tried to steady her Kinetic Honda, which was vibrating more due to human excitement than any mechanical malfunction.

'Yeah, yeah, imagine, how thrilled they are going to be! *Usha, I love you!*' I screamed into the air, and Pune's human traffic on wheels scowled, sniggered or laughed at us.

ॐ

'Yaayy!' screamed Arpita when we relayed the glad tidings.

But I was more interested in Jana's reaction. As usual, he was unemotional about it and continued to sip his beer nonchalantly. Arpi had wanted us to go to Blue Diamond for a latte or something, but he had declined, saying that one doesn't have to go anywhere to experience Paradise so we cancelled that plan.

'Jana, you don't seem to be too excited about Vishy's big break?' Usha's question seemed more of an accusation.

'Aren't you folks attaching too much importance to temporary, mundane events that will end with you? All this is mere dust, and the intelligent one doesn't feel elated or excited about getting a better breathing space within a dustbin,' said Jana, gazing intently at the neon lights rippling in the river below.

'Oho, he's been like this since today's White Lotus; don't mind him,' said Arpita.

'Balls! He was born this way. I guess he's just plain jealous of my success,' I said as Arpita and Usha left for the kitchen to whip up my fave late-night dessert, chilled mango milkshake.

They had always been rather unconcerned about my verbal tussles with him, of which there had been many.

'Vishy, grand emotions like jealousy are for unevolved minds like yours. What you call success is just a different kind of pain,' Jana started his lecture.

'Oh yeah? Damn your stupid pravachan. Go join some spiritual channel. You bloody boor, but for me you would have been living like a beggar at the Burning Ghat forever! *I* recommended you for the Cosmos job and *I* bought you clothes and *I* helped you move up in life...'

'You are pathetic, Vishy! You are stupid enough to be a great actor! The best liars make the best actors. Even animals act well. Go see any circus. So there is nothing great about all this. Think of your director as the ringmaster and yourself as a tamed lion.'

Jana was making sense, so I hated him all the more. Damn, what had come over me? Why was I even listening to him? I was going to become rich and famous and successful, so why was I even wishing that a worthless philosopher would acknowledge my achievement?

To hell with him, I thought. But what if he is right? Bah! He's just plain envious, forget it, money and fame make the world go round, not bullshit philosophy!

He was looking at the river—it was time to flow away from him.

'I don't care a damn about your opinion, Jana! I don't need your certificates on what I am and what I am not! Damn you, one day you will cry to me that you fucked up your life, mark my words!' I said, unable to restrain myself, despite some neat self-motivating thoughts.

'There you go again. What a nag! You always want to have the last word, don't you?' he sighed.

'Fuck you!' I shouted.

'Best you could come up with, huh? Golden words, indeed!' he said.

I left in a huff and sulked in my room. For 'sulked' read 'pondered long and hard' and you have the right picture.

Why did I want to break him? He had not harmed me in any way. Deep down, did I feel inferior to him? Did I feel inadequate every time I saw him in that deathly calm state? Wasn't he right? Was I not chasing meaningless stuff that had no ultimate bearing on one's levels of happiness?

LEVEL 13

The Pursuit of Happyness

You can use your tongue either as a weapon or as a balm.

Arpita had said yesterday that it was good to have a person like Jana around because it kept one so grounded. Emotional aberrations like excitement, elation and ecstasy were foolish traits, according to him.

Anyway, I was flying from another coop again and hoped that I wouldn't have to meet Jana for a while. I needed to get him off my mind. He had grown on me, taken possession of my mind and heart and been something of an intellectual sparring partner. But now, no more.

I would make new friends, whom I would *rule*. Enough was enough! Jana would no longer be my idol, my sounding board, my confidant or my guide. I would carve my own special place under the sun. No longer would I be second best and keep trying to outdo him...and fail. I would become so big that he would be totally dwarfed.

I focused on my golden future to delete depressing thoughts of eternal spiritual diamonds and all that crap.

ॐ

'I can't believe that you haven't told your folks yet,' rebuked Usha as we grabbed a late breakfast bite at Utsav.

'Hey, wait till the cheque gets cleared. I have just deposited it today, na?'

'What's the cheque got to do with your conveying the good news to your parents?'

'Stupid, what if the cheque bounces? What if Harry cancels the contract?'

'Huh? How can he? He can be dragged to court!'

'Bull! We are nothing compared to Bawa and Harry. Not yet, at least. They are rich and have awesome contacts. They can have me for breakfast any given day.'

'Okay, you have a point. So should we go to Cosmos or not? I thought we will stop from today, go on sick leave or something.'

'Of course we will go. It will be more fun, something like a swan song. Let's just chill out, and we can talk to Duniya on Thursday about whether Cosmos will waive the notice period and all.'

'Shit! Completely skipped my mind. We have to give them one month's notice, or one month's salary. What do we do?'

'Arre, don't worry about that. If the cheque gets cleared, we will pay Cosmos. I will pay for both of us, okay? And if it doesn't, we will continue. Cool?'

'Done, superstar!'

'Q2, thanks for being so understanding about my scenes with Nimika—'

'Q2? What's that?'

'Take a wild guess! New term to symbolize our new life!'

'Queen 2? Meaning that Nimika is Queen 1?'

'No, stupid.'

'Oh, you mean your mom is Queen 1 in your life and I am Queen 2; that's okay!'

'Arre, no, Q doesn't stand for queen...it is a term of endearment...think harder...'

'I am too excited to figure out anything now!'

'Stupid, it is an extension of *cute.*'

'Ooooohhh! How sweet!'

'You really don't mind my scenes with Nimika, na?'

'Arre, no jaanu. To be an actor, you have to cavort with the actresses. Is there any other way? I love you too much to worry about your professional celluloid intimacy. In fact, I love you so much that even if you sleep with someone and you're happy about it, then I'll be happy about your happiness...'

'Never! I can't even think of any other woman, Usha. You were, are and will always be the only lady in my life. I'd rather die than make love to anyone else.'

୬

Ah, what I really loved about Usha was her 'I am a basics person' attitude. The day after the cheque was cleared, I suggested we go to Meridien to grab an expensive, exotic buffet. She nixed my idea, so we went to Just Paranthas. I kept looking at the janata around us, wondering how many of them would eventually become my fans. Who knew, perhaps I wouldn't be able to dine out at open eateries like these ever again, if Nimika was to be believed.

I chuckled inwardly and burped a burp of pompous satisfaction. Suddenly, I felt I was a magical cut above the rest already, and enjoyed looking down upon the crowd around.

'But always pretend to be humble,' I chanted to myself as I chomped down the stuffed parantha. 'Keep mouthing diplomatic lies that you will never mean. Never get into controversies. Never take a stand on any subject. Never reveal your mind to the media. Camouflage your crooked thoughts behind apparently straightforward comments...' (Wasn't I becoming good in the art of deception that would eventually get immortalized as media interviews? Wow! I think I really fell in love with myself at that moment!)

'Okay, now we call up your folks,' said Usha.

'Not now, later,' I said.

'Why?' she asked as I settled the bill.

'Today's a national holiday, Mom would have gone to the temple with her friends,' I said, not wishing to divulge the real reason for not wanting to make that call: Dad would be at home and I was in no mood to talk to him.

'Call on her cell,' she said.

'Forget it, she must be busy singing bhajans at the temple. You know it's really beautiful, there is a huge statue of Lord Krishna—' I said.

'Stop digressing, I am calling up your home,' she said, yanking away my cell, and punched the speed dial and speakerphone function.

'Usha...please...'

'Shut up. Hmm... It's ringing...perhaps you are right... they don't seem to be at home.'

'Told you. Now hang up.'

'Hey...your mom picked up...here, talk...' she whispered gleefully.

Darn! Mom was at home? I'd also have to speak with the old man? After the initial pleasantries were exchanged and I told her about my lucky break, Mom screamed.

'What's she saying?' asked Usha in a low voice.

'She's telling Dad that I am going to become a film star...' I translated.

'Very good, very good,' said Mom to me. 'I always knew you would finally become somebody one day...didn't I tell you?'

'Mamma, I also have a girlfriend now,' I said, wanting to divert attention to something more probable and certain. (Who knew? Perhaps the film would be a dud and I would become a laughing stock. Was I already suffering the famed insecurity virus that haunts celebs? Anyway, I was conveying a subtle message that I was finally taking charge of my life.)

'Girlfriend? Who?' asked Mom.

'Talk to her yourself...very nice person...I see a lot of you in her, Mamma,' I said.

'Hello, Auntyji, how are you? I am Usha.'

'Usha...nice name, beta...how long you have known him? And how did all this happen?' asked Mom.

'Auntyji, I was Vishy's team leader at the call centre... and slowly, we came closer—' said Usha shyly.

'Oh, okay...good...good...' said Mom hesitantly. 'Tell Vishy his papa wants to talk to him.'

'Films are for cretins and corrupted minds. What is this film star thing you are getting into now?' Dad said accusatorily in his thundering baritone, as if I was planning a bank robbery or something.

'Papa, I got a role in a film, a Hindi film. Shooting will begin next week...' I explained.

'What's the role?' he asked.

'Hero,' I said.

'Hero? Are you sure? They must have said villain or extra, and you must have wrongly heard hero,' he said sarcastically.

'C'mon, Papa, I just signed a contract, they are paying me ten lakh,' I said.

'Ten lakh? I make that in a year! How long will you work for the film?' he enquired. (No congratulations! No joy! No nothing! Some folk just don't change!)

'Three months or so,' I said.

'Okay, and what is this girlfriend thing?' he asked. 'I told you, Pune girls will ruin you.' (Third accusation — and I was keeping count.)

'Papa, she's a very nice person, Mom just spoke to her,' I said, angry that I still had to sound defensive in his presence, telephonic or otherwise.

'Your mom will find anyone nice! She will even tie Gabbar Singh a rakhi,' he sneered. (Fourth accusation.)

'Uncle, I am not all that bad!' laughed Usha.

'Huh? Who's that?' Dad's tone changed to surprise.

I didn't tell him that the speakerphone was on, but he was too sharp not to have guessed when Usha butted in. I hoped that my old man would at least get embarrassed about his catty comments and make me happy at having caught him off-guard for once. He disappointed me by displaying more sangfroid than I could ever manage to marshal.

'Uncle, I am Usha, Vishy's girlfriend.'

'Hmmm? Okay, so what is your full name?' asked Dad in a tone that surely suggested that he wished to make amends for having cast generic aspersions on a complete stranger. (He was good at PR, wasn't he?)

'Usha Tripathi, Uncle.'

'Tripathi? Hmmm...UP?' he asked. (The guy was smart! He had managed a friendly, diplomatic, placatory tone in a matter of nanoseconds. I made a mental note of it. The tonal variation might come in useful in some future movie.)

'Yes Uncle, UP Brahmin, we are pucca vegetarians.'

'That is good, non-veg people will go to hell and be reborn as the very animals they eat; it is clearly written in our holy scriptures,' he said righteously. (Suddenly our common enemy was not 'wanton Pune girls' but 'flesh-eaters'. No wonder he had climbed the banking ladder pretty fast, thanks to his uncanny ability to move from tyrant to tactician in the blink of an eye.)

'Yes, Uncle, and my dad is a professor at a university—' said Usha.

'Good, good, teaching is a very noble profession...what does he teach?'

'English literature to postgraduates, Uncle.'

'Excellent! You know, I have also done English, though I have forgotten most of Shakespeare and Milton and Byron,' said Dad rather pompously.

'It shows, Uncle, you have good command over the language. Vishy keeps praising you...' said Usha.

'I am sure he never does anything like that. So tell me, what are your plans, Usha?'

'Plans, Uncle?' wondered Usha.

'I mean romantic plans,' Dad explained.

'Uncle, we are...we are just getting to know each other and all; we are close, but we have not done...I mean ours is a very *healthy* relationship...we are good friends only,' she stuttered, clearly taken aback by his pointed query.

'Nothing physical yet, you mean? I am a modern man, you can talk freely with me...even Vishy's mom and I, we had a love marriage, though we are both Bengalis, we came from different castes...big jhamela happened between both families but we fought it out...and you know, Vishy is more like a north Indian...knows better Hindi than Bengali,' said Dad, making Usha feel at ease.

'Yes, Uncle...Vishy is good—'

'Well, Usha, you seem to be a nice girl, come over to Delhi sometime, and do your parents know about you people?'

'Only Dad. I lost my mom when I was six. Dad knows about Vishy and says that I should take my own decisions—'

'Oh, I am so sorry, Usha, about your mom. You would like to marry Vishy?'

'I guess so, Uncle...eventually...'

'Good, I am all for love marriage... Okay, talk to Vishy's mom, your mother-in-law to be,' laughed Dad.

'Hello Auntyji!' said Usha.

'Should I call you bahu now? How serious is this?' asked Mom.

'Arre, Mamma—' I interjected.

'Keep quiet, I am talking to my bahu,' said Mom.

'Auntyji, we both are in...in...' stammered Usha.

'Love?' suggested Mom.

'Yes, Auntyji!' said Usha, relieved.

'Good, what's there to be shy about then? Love is divine, beta. You promise to take care of my Vishy?' (What a clichéd question! As if someone could say 'no' to that.)

'Of course, Auntyji!'

'Then he is all yours. Like kanyadaan, there should also be putradaan. Since it is a modern era, I donate you my boy, and let us do the marriage right now on the telephone itself...' said Mom jocularly.

'Arre, Mamma, first let me get settled,' I protested.

'Okay, what's the name of the film?' asked Dad.

'*Paisa To Gul Total Cool.*'

'What sort of a crazy name is that?' he wondered aloud. (Fifth accusation.)

'This is what works in the market, it is a comedy script,' I said.

'Okay, so Usha will be in Pune and you will be in Mumbai?' he asked.

'No, she is also coming with me, the producer is giving us a flat in Andheri...later, we'd like to move to Bandra... though Andheri is cheaper...' I said.

'Yes, Bandra is more posh...good...so you are going to have a live-in relationship... No problem...but you must marry Usha only, okay? Love is sacred. You should not ditch her, it is time you learned some responsibility,' Dad rebuked. (Sixth accusation.)

'Okay Papa, have to meet some friends, plus, there's lots of work... Talk to you later,' I said hurriedly.

'Okay, say bye to your mom...at least learn some telephone etiquette,' he said. (Seventh accusation.)

'Bye, Mamma!' I shouted.

'Bye, dear, and Usha, my blessings, beta, always trust in God,' said Mom.

'Thank you, Auntyji!' said Usha.

'Happy?' I asked Usha as I disconnected the call, quite peeved that talking to Dad always made me squirm a bit, and also left a bad taste...on my ego.

'They are such wonderful people!' she exclaimed.

'*They*? Yeah, Mom is good, but the old man...'

'I don't know why you don't like him.'

'Of course not! He's a bully. Didn't you see how he came up with hazaar accusations in a span of minutes?'

'Vishy, he means well, that's just his style.'

'Forget him. I don't want to spoil my wonderful mood thinking about him.'

'Cool. Did Harry or Nimika call regarding our flat?'

'No, not yet, but it's not our problem. If the shooting has to begin in time, they have to find something fast...of course, it will have to match our newfound status and all, the ball is in their court now.' (Ah, wasn't I beginning to talk like a film star already?)

'Yeah, and we have the money too... Jaanu, I am so happy for us... We are simple people, so we simply deserve the best!' (Ah, wasn't she also adding the much-needed fragrance of arrogance to my starry airs? *Ram milayi jodi.* Good! If you are humble and easygoing, the world usually swallows you up or uses you for wall-to-wall carpeting.)

'Quite right. Q2, promise me that you will always love me!'

'You want me to tattoo your name on my hand or something?'

ॐ

Another good thing was that Duniya waived our notice period, eliciting a promise from me that I would one day return the favour by doing a free endorsement, and by participating in a recruitment drive for Cosmos. That suited us just fine. What was the harm in promising anything in the present, if you could eventually wriggle out of it one day in the future by citing your busy schedule?

The last day at Cosmos saw Arpita organizing a booze party on our office terrace. I was getting progressively drunk by the minute, and nearly everyone extracted a promise from me that I'd invite them to the premiere of my debut movie.

Jana was sitting all by himself and I let him be.

I was in no mood to talk to him—was I creating a wedge between us deliberately? Perhaps. But who cared?

The rolling stone gathers no boss. You can't drive forward if you keep staring at the rearview mirror.

Why did I always end up regurgitating Jana's pet statements whenever I imbibed some alcohol?

Oh, I forgot to tell you, but I began drinking a month ago, when Arpita forced a bit of red wine on me, saying that perfect moderation was more difficult than perfect abstinence. Plus, she had convinced me by saying that I should practise the art of social drinking to hobnob with the party animals and celebs who would eventually become my colleagues and contemporaries.

Rising Sun

*Thinking about what others think of
you is a Bollywood pastime.*

Harry had got us a nice 2 BHK at Royal Harmony Apartments in Lokhandwala, Andheri. Nimika chipped in with the interior decoration, and the first week of our migration to Mumbai saw us settling down bit by bit, though I must confess that I missed the laid-back serenity of Pune.

Usha was happy to see me being given the royal treatment by my employers as we began living in. No, we didn't sleep with each other, and had decided to reserve hardcore physical intimacy for some post-marital day. To that extent, we were quite conservative, which suited both of us just fine, since we had decided to focus on our respective careers for now.

Lokhandwala and its surrounds were quite happening places indeed. Malls, multiplexes and the ubiquitous McDonald's relayed a subliminal message that we had arrived, that we were successful, that I was about to become the new happening face of Bollywood.

Nimika used to come over almost every other day to familiarize me with the script, and to guide Usha on everything from 'the best VFM beauty parlour' and 'the best leggings, tops and women's accessories shop, The Queen's Gambit' to 'the best chaat joint, Kiroriwala.'

After a week, Harry said that the shooting had been postponed by a few days due to 'circumstances beyond our control.' (I later gathered that one financier had walked out of the project, but Bawa had been astute enough to fall back on a contingency plan by mortgaging his sprawling ancestral property in south Delhi.)

So there was a lot of pressure to make the movie a hit and recover the money spent; in fact, Harry and Bawa kept insisting that Nimika and I get to know the script better than the back of our hands. We rehearsed our scenes diligently and Usha recorded them on Harry's handycam, so that he could give us tips on how to improve and look more natural.

Life was fun.

The food was great—Guru da Dhaba at Lokhandwala served the best rajma in the subcontinent.

The shopping was fantastic—Nimika doubled up as a dress designer (rather, buyer) and we picked up lots of good outfits for me, both casuals and formals.

The romance was wonderful—Usha gave me a massage every night before I went to sleep, and I returned the favour whenever she allowed me to.

ॐ

The mahurat shot happened at a bungalow in Madh Island. This place would function as my office, advertising agency and home in the movie. It had taken them about a fortnight to design the sets. We had booked the place for about a month, and Bawa said that he had chosen this venue because it also had a swimming pool, where Nimika and I would soon be doing our semi-naked cavorting scenes. The water in the pool was quite murky, but Harry promised that it would be cleaned up in a day or two.

The pundit kept chanting some esoteric mantras while pouring ghee into a havan kund.

'Okay, time for the mahurat shot!' yelled Bawa into the microphone, checking his monitor.

'Lights!'

The lights bathed Nimika and me in incredible heat. I took a deep breath. This was my moment in history. My first official step into the hallowed portals of Bollywood!

'Camera!' screamed Harry.

'Rolling!' shouted the cameraman.

'Action!' yelled Harry.

Both Nimika and I melted into our roles. The world disappeared. A new world had appeared. And I had merged into it. No, seriously. Harry once said: 'Enjoy life as if it's a fake movie; act in a movie as if you are enjoying real life.' I hadn't understood him then. Now, I did. This is the hallmark of all great actors. The actor vanishes; only the character remains. We flowed through the scene effortlessly...

'Cut!' said Harry. 'Hurrah! Well done! Well done!'

The entire unit clapped, giving us a standing ovation.

'Single take! These people are single-take actors, whew!' roared Bawa.

'Congrats, Vishy, brilliant take!' said Nimika, punching me on the shoulder.

'Ditto, Nimika,' I replied. 'You were remarkable, too!'

Usha gave me a big hug and whispered something like, 'You are a born actor, Vishy, you are as muted as Dilip Kumar and as dashing as Amitabh Bachchan...she was good too, but on the monitor, you looked better...'

'Cool, Usha, thanks!' I said, landing a peck on her cheek.

We all gathered around the monitor and the scene was replayed a billion times. I felt as tall as Mount Everest, as if I had reached the summit of a new life, though it had just begun.

Nearly everyone back-thumped me, congratulating me on my performance. There is nothing like collective appreciation to make you feel good about yourself. I was feeing so damn happy, I could have fallen in love with my worst enemy.

This is the life, I thought, this is called success. Balls to Jana. Bloody nutcase, why are you thinking of Jana now? Forget that loser-turned-philosopher...

We shot till about 5 p.m. and Usha got really bored. She whispered to me that this was the last shoot she was going to accompany me to, and I felt pretty happy about it—having someone you know at a shoot can make you feel so self-conscious and inhibited.

Plus, Usha had just got an offer from Mind Wind, a call centre at Malad that serviced domestic banks and credit card customers, so she would become busy soon, and would certainly not have enough time to attend shoots.

Anyway, my maiden day went off well, and though Harry and Bawa insisted that we celebrate the occasion by popping champagne at the Marriot after pack up, I declined the invite.

∿

'So, how long will it be before the movie is released?' asked Usha as she began the customary bedtime massage.

'Ummm,' I murmured, 'maybe about two to three months of shooting, then a fortnight or so of dubbing and all, plus add a month for post-production and publicity. They are planning to do it fast.'

'You think it will be a hit?'

'Who knows? The script's funny, yes, but you know, one can never really gauge the taste of the audience. Though Harry is confident that I will be received well—he says I have a great sense of comic timing...'

'He's just flattering you.'

'Yeah? And what is there to be gained by that?'

'Flattery will keep you happy, and that way you will give it your hundred per cent.'

'As if you didn't like my acting...'

'I didn't say that; you are good, though there is scope for improvement.'

'Meri ma, there always is, I will become better and better, no doubt, but I am definitely a far more accomplished actor than I thought I was.'

'You don't need Harry for flattery—you are doing such a good job of it yourself.'

'Shut up, let's sleep now, long day tomorrow. Goodnight, Q2.'

'Goodnight, honey.'

ꝏ

If you need good pre-launch publicity for your movie in the making, then you have to hobnob with the media, the PR guys and the who's who of Bollywood.

Thanks to Harry's experience in making TVCs (television commercials) he knew quite a few pillars of our make-believe, hype-and-hoopla world.

The filmy parties he arranged nearly every month were graced by several socialites. 'We have to constantly be on Page 3...' Nimika whispered to me as she pecked some yucky-looking, drowned-in-jewellery bearded man. 'Nothing like keeping the socialites and newspaper folk in good humour to become a success story.'

But Usha didn't like the parties, the highfalutin fashion tips and gossip talk of the socialites, so I had to go all by myself.

Bawa said that it would not be good PR if Usha kept saying stuff like 'these silly losers carry more gas within them than LPG cylinders' within earshot of the media guys. I was actually glad that she mostly chose to stay back, or drive down to her call centre to sort out some late-night glitch.

Usha had now bought a Santro for herself on EMI, and I was happy with the pick-and-drop facility provided by Harry for my shoots and other social occasions.

After about three months, our movie was nearly complete. We had dubbed for it, added sound effects, edited it a bit and we now had a rough cut. I asked Harry if my family could take a look and he was kind enough to arrange a preview at Dimple theatre in Bandra.

This was the first time my folks would meet their prospective bahu. Usha was going crazy, and taking sartorial advice from Nimika. They were bonding rather well and that was a good sign. It is just great if a hero's wife is friendly with a heroine who does intimate and passionate scenes with him—that prevents domestic turmoil actually.

Nimika suggested that Usha wear something 'semi-modern and acceptably chic', like leggings and a kurti, and top off her attire with traditional Kolhapuri slippers, traditional nosering and earrings, and also carry an uber-modern clutch, coming across as a modern bahu with traditional values. It set me back financially by a few thousands, but I didn't mind, since parental approval wouldn't exactly hurt our relationship.

When we picked up Mom and Dad from the airport, Usha solemnly and smilingly namasted them, just like air hostesses do—only Usha appeared less fake—and also touched my parents' feet. Mom and Dad were obviously happy at this traditional display of servility and humility.

Dad approvingly said to her, 'Trust today's women to respect age-old traditions that are the basic bulwark of our evolved religion and society,' and throwing a glaring look at me, 'but some modern, useless men can't be expected to carry forward time-honoured customs into Kali Yuga.'

Mom said, 'You started again? Arre, Vishy respects us and loves us, but doesn't like to keep displaying it publicly, right Vishy?'

Some things never change, I thought.

I think I nodded both yes and no to Mom's observation as I silently pushed their trolley towards the parking lot.

Both of them liked Usha, though—I could clearly read

that in their eyes and smiles—and that's what was important. Mom had already developed a soft corner for her when she'd heard that Usha had lost her mother during childhood and Dad was always a sucker for fake humility.

'So when's the premiere? Tomorrow? We will be leaving Sunday evening. Lots of work at the bank. Tomorrow is Sunday, if you have become literate enough to read calendars,' Dad said to me as I revved up the Santro.

'It's a *preview*, Papa, not premiere, that will happen later—'

'Yes, yes, preview only, don't try to throw cinematic jargon at me, you understood what I meant!'

'It's scheduled for tomorrow afternoon, and your flight is at 10 p.m., so we will have plenty of time,' I said.

'So, Vishy,' said Mom, 'how was your maiden experience?'

'*Maiden* experience indeed! With a maiden called Nimika, right?' interjected Dad. 'Nobody makes religious movies these days based on *Bhagavatam*, there's a treasure trove of stories in them but who cares, all they want are item numbers that pollute the minds of today's youth...'

'Uncle,' said Usha, 'Nimika is a nice girl. In fact, she and I are good friends now, but you are right, the audience decides the kinds of movies that happen, and the producers have to give them titillating songs and scenes to keep them happy.'

'A good creative person should try to influence and change collective, depraved thought patterns, Usha, not just purvey prurient goods in the name of modern cinema. Semi-naked dances, lewd dialogues and perverted producers and actresses have ruined Indian cinema permanently,' replied Dad.

'You are right, Uncle, but Bollywood is where the money is,' reasoned Usha.

'Money is not everything. Character is more important. Money will go. But values will stay with one's soul eternally. So many talented people don't become actors only because the modern cinematic atmosphere is so corrupted. If I were the PM, I would ban all films and TV shows which you can't bear to see with your kids. Why can't they make more family-oriented movies?' he argued.

'Vishy speaks very highly of your principles,' said Usha, diverting his attention from bare-all, dare-all Bollywood masala.

'I am sure he says I am highly idiotic, autocratic and pedantic,' said Dad.

How did he guess that one?

'Please, let's just enjoy Vishy's newfound success. He can't help it if we are no longer in the Sampoorna Ramayana era. People want entertainment and even entertainment is a service to humanity,' said Mom.

'Hmm... Why is there so much traffic? Delhi roads are so much better. Only idiots settle down in Mumbai,' Dad changed track.

Thankfully, the focus had shifted from Bollywood-bashing to Mumbai-bashing.

'Very unplanned, very chaotic, the invention of the internal combustion engine by Karl Benz, I think in the 1880s, has ruined our cities and towns today... Just goes to prove that the past can devastate the future...it is the past that controls the future...' whinged Dad.

'Uncle, you are so knowledgeable,' said Usha, flattering his pomposity.

'One should always carry knowledge lightly,' beamed Dad, and turning slightly towards me, 'but some even carry ignorance heavy-headedly.'

When would we reach our pad? I was dying to get away from this guy. Not a word of congratulations on my debut movie! Not a word of appreciation! Did he realize how difficult it is to make it in Bollywood? One in a million even gets a slim chance and a decent break. Then you need to have the talent to sustain your filmy career. You need to work hard, no, slog, dance and sing in the rain and the midday sun, apply itchy greasepaint, memorize reams of dialogues, dub for them later... Sheesh, it is more gruelling torture than glamorous tamasha...most days it seemed as if I was working in a Bangladeshi sweatshop, only we weren't churning out jute handbags but movies...

Calm down, Vishy. Dad was born with a cynical chromosomal pattern. Not his fault. Act cool, you are good at that!

॥

Mom and Usha loved the movie. Dad hated it.

But I was happy that Dad mumbled 'good' rather gracelessly when Harry and Nimika asked him about it. Diplomacy was still his forte—unless he was talking to us in private.

'Vishy, how can you unhook a girl's bra on screen? Don't you have any shame?' Dad stormed as I slid the Santro out of the parking lot at Dimple.

'Uncle, he had told me about it!' said Usha.

'That doesn't justify taking part in a sleazy skinfest. All those bikini scenes and raunchy numbers were just not needed! And how can you kiss a girl to earn money?' he shouted.

Mom remained silent; so did I.

'But, Uncle, the comedy was good, no?' said Usha. 'And what do you think about Vishy's acting?'

'Yes, at times, the comedy was interesting, and Vishy did better than I expected him to,' said Dad grudgingly.

Interesting? The comedy was a few notches above even *Chashme Buddoor*. Better than expected? I was better than Govinda! When will the old man give me the credit and appreciation I so richly deserve? Some people are so miserly when it comes to dishing out compliments.

'So, Usha, when are you coming to Delhi? I will teach you a few Bengali cooking tricks,' said Mom.

'Definitely someday, Aunty, when Vishy is free,' smiled Usha.

'When are you getting married?' asked Dad.

'We haven't decided,' said Usha.

'Okay, we will match your horoscope, and do some puja or something, if there is some problem. Also, I will have to talk to your father,' said Dad.

'He already knows about Vishy, and that we are staying together—'

'All that is okay, but still, elders can't be bypassed,' Dad cut in.

'Absolutely, Uncle, I am happy that you approve of me anyway,' said Usha.

'Approve of you? Of course we approve. But what you saw in Vishy beats me. Perhaps you like a simpleton who believes in simple thinking and high living,' said Dad.

'C'mon Uncle, stop ribbing Vishy, he's got a golden heart,' protested Usha.

'If you say so,' laughed Dad.

Our preview had got delayed, as some Bollywood bigshot had pulled rank and booked Dimple theatre for his family in the afternoon. So we didn't have much time left to reach the airport after we had finished watching my movie. I hate cutting it fine, but there had been no choice.

I drove as fast as Mumbai traffic would allow me, as I didn't have enough energy left in me to tolerate Dad anymore if he missed the flight.

We saw off Mom and Dad rather hurriedly and Usha did the servility thing once more. I hugged Mom and waved a weak goodbye to Dad. He just nodded slightly and walked off.

'Phew!' I said as they disappeared.

'You look so relieved, Vishy!' said Usha.

'You would too, if you were a cabbage brain with a cynical critic for a dad.'

'He has a lovely sense of humour.'

'Yeah, nasty sarcasm is sometimes mistaken for that.'

'Quite brainy, too.'

'Why don't you write a thesis on him? You seem to know more about him than me!'

'I will, one day. Actually he's a sweetheart, and quite a personality.'

'Thanks for loving the person I hate.'

'Hate is just love standing upside-down.'

'Whatever. Anyway, dinner kahan? I'm famished.'

'Legacy of China. That is, if you can afford it.'

'Not after you splurged on stupid clothes and jewellery to impress them—'

'But they liked me, na?'

'After having a son like me, anyone will like a person like you.'

'Stop being so harsh on yourself. Your failed teenage life is over now.'

'Somehow, Dad will never let me forget that.'

'Grow up, Vishy, or else you will grow into a grouchy middle-aged monster in the coming years.'

'I am not grouchy. But every time I meet him, he makes me feel so inadequate. Just like Jana—'

'Forget all that now. We are together, we are happening, we have arrived, so step on the gas, dump the past and zoom into the future!'

I did just that.

LEVEL 15

Turbulence

*Loving someone means giving them
the right to hurt you.*

Our first argument took place a fortnight later,
when Usha didn't come home one night. Well,
at least not on time. Usually, she was expected at
around 9 p.m., since she worked from 11 a.m. to 8 p.m.
most days.

I reached our pad at 8.45 p.m. after an early pack up,
when we reshot some minor scene that Bawa hadn't been
happy about at the preview, and I was getting increasingly
angry and worried that I couldn't reach Usha over the phone
even by 10 p.m. I kept calling Usha's cell every five minutes.
*The mobile phone you are trying to reach is currently switched
off. Please try again later.* I must have heard that message a
million times. Then I got frantic. I tried a few numbers she
had given me—her VP, some colleague, and the landline at
the call centre. All were either busy or switched off. What
had happened? Accident? Hope she was okay...

I decided to wait for a while. If she doesn't return in another hour, I'll take an auto to her call centre, I thought... I must have dozed off on a wave of worry and despair...

Someone shook me awake.

It was Usha.

'What time is it?' I asked angrily.

'Arre, why are you snapping at me?' she said.

'What time is it?'

'3 a.m.'

'Is this the time to come home? Why was your cell switched off? Where were you?'

'Vishy, stop it, okay? I am not your slave. Do I ever ask you why you come home late from your parties?'

'So you were at a party?'

'Yes.'

'Where?'

'Listen, I am tired, need to sleep, we'll talk tomorrow!'

'No, we will talk now! Enough is enough!'

'Calm down, why are you getting so worked up?'

'Worked up? I have been trying to reach you forever! I was so worried, and you don't have the basic courtesy to call and say you will be late?'

'I texted you, okay?'

'I didn't get any text.'

'That's not my fault! Sometimes SMSes don't reach.'

'Why couldn't you call me?'

'I did. At around 7 p.m. Your cell was switched off.'

'I was shooting at Madh Island, but that's not the point.'

'Then what is?'

'Listen, Usha, *this is the last time*! If you are ever late again and don't tell me where you are and with whom, then...then...'

'Then what? What will you do? Stop threatening me, Vishy. I am not your bloody slave—'

'You will do as I say!'

'Balls! I will do nothing of the sort. From now on, neither do you need to tell me anything, nor will I!'

'Where were you?'

'I told you, I am not saying anything!'

'Are you having an affair?'

'How dare you!'

'Okay, Usha, I am asking calmly, where were you?'

'Python.'

'Disc?'

'Yeah.'

'With whom?'

'With my team, to motivate them, that's why you couldn't reach us there! You know, na, cells don't work within Python...'

'With whom?'

'You don't believe me?'

'Was Vineet with you?'

'You called Vineet?'

'Yeah, his cell was switched off, too!'

'No, he wasn't with us...and what's come over you? Are you suspecting me of infidelity?'

'No, I am suspecting you of lying...'

'Meaning you think I was not at Python...'

'Yeah.'

'Damn you, Vishy! I owe you no explanation!'

'*Yes, you do!*' I screamed as I slapped her.

'You barbarian!' she shouted and stormed off.

'You bloody bitch!'

We slept in different bedrooms.

No bedtime massage for me.

అ

The next morning we made our own individual breakfasts. Darn, even the cook-cum-maid hadn't arrived. I didn't have any shoot or dubbing or meeting to go to and was feeling guilty for what I had done. (Yeah, she'd been at Python with her team—I confirmed that by calling up the DJ, whom I knew, early in the morning.)

I shouldn't have slapped her. This was the first time I had done something so primitive. 'And this should be the last time you behave like a brute—domestic violence is just not the done thing, Vishy,' I told myself.

'Listen, Q2, I am sorry, guess I was angry that you had me so worried last night, plus I was disappointed, had great plans for us for the evening...' I said as she walked out of the kitchen.

She didn't reply. Obviously she wasn't buying the argument.

'Okay, my fault, I apologize,' I said as I settled down at the dining table.

She took away her plate and walked into the living room.

'Suit yourself. How long can you not talk to me?' I said after her.

She finished her breakfast, bathed, got dressed and was preparing to leave for her office.

'Listen, Q2, can't you take the day off? I am totally free today, and I want to make it up to you,' I pleaded.

'No need to, stop feeling guilty, it's okay,' she replied, adjusting her collar.

'Sorry. Say you have forgiven me.'

'Listen, Vishy, I am not angry that you slapped me, but suspecting me of lying and infidelity is something I just can't stomach...'

'Hey,' I said, enveloping her from behind as she sat at the dressing table mirror, 'it will never happen again! So sorry!'

'Okay, accepted,' she said. 'But I can't take the day off, just because you are free!'

'That's okay, we will have a lovely candlelight dinner at Olive—shall I make a reservation?'

'No, I guess I will be late again tonight...'

'*Again?* Another party?'

'No, we have this hotshot client who loves to meet over dinner at the Taj; don't come prying around, I'll be in Bandra only, at the Lands End...'

'Usha, this is too much! You don't even need to work for this lousy forty or fifty grand! I will make enough money for both of us...'

'Shut up, Vishy! Don't put me off early in the morning. I need to be financially independent. I can't afford to have you treat me like a doormat and a parasite feasting off your moolah!'

'*Our* moolah! What is mine is also yours, Q2!'

'And what am I supposed to do after quitting my job?'

'Well, just chill out, manage our pad, manage my travels, accompany me on my shoots, go shopping, whatever.'

'Basically be a maidservant—what is euphemistically known as "homemaker"—and be your secretary, and live like a gangster's moll living off his spoils, right?'

'You are making it sound crude. Is my mom a maidservant and a moll?'

'Don't bring your mom into it. We are a different generation. And you are not your dad. He has more respect for her than you will ever have for me!'

'Hey, that's not true! I love and respect you, Usha, it is just that we can spend more quality time together...'

'And let my life revolve around yours? You want me to be your satellite? Sorry to disappoint you, Vishy, I will never sacrifice my freedom and let you ride roughshod over me!'

'Please think about it, Usha.'

'Never. End of discussion. Or you be the homemaker, and we can survive on the ₹50,000 or more that I will eventually earn. I will make you an offer. You sit at home. I will earn for both of us. Accepted?'

'Just because you are two years older it doesn't make you wiser. Stop mothering me!'

'Don't digress. Why don't you sit at home and live off me?'

'C'mon, don't talk nonsense!'

'Ditto!'

ॐ

Usha and I had been so happy in Pune. And in Mumbai, we were living like two ambitious go-getters trying to make our marks in our respective careers. We were like an alpha male and an alpha female who didn't actually need anyone in their lives. There is something strange about Mumbai's very atmosphere and vibes. Everyone is running around trying to reach somewhere. Everyone is so busy with themselves that they live life in fast motion. Everyone has some impossible goals. (I wanted to be India's No. 1 film star. Usha aspired to be her call centre's CEO in four years. Even my maid had ambitions of buying a kholi in Bandra.) Everyone is on the go. But nobody knows where they are going. This is Mumbai. Here, life passes you by while you are busy doing other things.

I began to discover that Usha and I were as similar as apples and oranges. I was a bit of a homebody; Usha was a regular at her 'team outings'. I didn't like to socialize much, unless it was for a professional reason; Usha loved to hang out with her call centre buddies—more for personal than professional reasons, though she never admitted it. I liked to watch movies at home; Usha preferred curling up with a book. I loved to celebrate our festivals; Usha hated all of them, saying 'all these festivals are just an excuse to go shopping or get drunk...for a wise person, life itself is a festival.'

Chalk and cheese;
Vishy, bear it please,
Think of nothing but the movie's release.

Bawa had arranged for Nimika and me to be picked up by a hired Merc limo.

Usha refused to attend the premiere, saying that she didn't like the filmy crowd, the constant camera flashlights and gossip columnists.

I would have loved it if Arpita could have been there, but she had gone to Baroda as her mom was unwell. Of course, I wasn't in touch with Jana any longer, and there was no point inviting someone who would just say that all this is maya and totally inconsequential.

Vishy, forget all that please; focus, instead, on what you will say.

This is your big day, the moment of truth; the past is far away...

'You are lost in thought...what's the matter? Butterflies in your stomach?' cooed Nimika as she placed a comforting hand on my thigh.

'Yeah, I am thinking of Usha and my old friends, and wondering how easily life has cast me into an altogether different dimension. It all seems so sudden and weird. From a nonentity to a celebrity...'

'It happens. You are destiny's child. Now savour your moment, dissolve into it, you are in the big league now. Forget them. Fate wants you to move ahead, so focus on that.'

LEVEL 16

The Deceivers

Controversies ought to pay entertainment tax.

The flashlights were blinding. As I stepped out of the limo, arguing with Nimika, I barely saw Harry and Bawa smiling widely at the throng that had gathered.

'This is *my* movie!' I shouted angrily at Nimika as I got off.

'It will do well only because of *my* oomph factor!' she shouted back.

The media guys were confused, but were happy that we were providing some real-life drama.

We both walked along the red carpet like knights busy in a verbal duel.

'Vishy! Vishy!' screamed an anchor as many cameras trained on me.

'Nimika! Just one sec!' screamed others who were more interested in interviewing the sexy babe in the see-through light pink gown.

We were standing just two feet from each other: ready to grab attention with our sound bytes.

'So Vishy, what were you saying?' asked an anchor.

'Look, a movie rides on a hero's talent, right? The heroine is just the glamour quotient. You can have movies without heroines but never without heroes, right?' I said.

'How very MCPish,' remarked a female anchor.

'Exactly!' assented Nimika. 'This guy is so full of himself! I am sick and tired of his narcissism. He's obsessed with himself!'

The media guys were having a field day. Forgotten were the other celebs who had gathered. Forgotten were the Bollywood badshahs Harry had invited. Forgotten was even the movie. They were covering nothing but the Vishy vs. Nimika slanging match.

'Listen Nimika, it is only because of *my* comic timing that the public will love it,' I said.

'Nonsense. A movie is not a game of solitaire. It is a team effort!' she returned.

'I agree,' I said, 'but in any team, some are more equal than others!'

'What about the scriptwriter and the director? Vishy, you're talking so much like Sarwin Narang,' remarked an anchor.

'Sarwin Narang is yesterday. He's as interesting as ancient ruins. I am leagues ahead of him. I am the today, the tomorrow, and the day after,' I retorted.

'You have not even yet begun and you are already so arrogant!' screamed Nimika. 'Ever heard of something called humility?'

'Humility is for the mediocre, for the wannabes. The people will love me, just you watch,' I said proudly.

'Vishy, are you saying that Harry is nothing, too? This movie could have been made without him?' asked an anchor, eager to stir up more controversy.

'Of course! Who are these guys Harry and Bawa anyway? Glorified ad film-makers. I agree the script is good, and that is courtesy Mayank Sharma. Any KG kid could have directed this script well. The screenplay is by Mayank and Balraj Khanna; those guys are the geniuses. The technicians, editors, cameramen, cinematographers, art directors, singers, music directors—they are the ones who have done a fantastic job. But these partners at Train Ticket Films are just pathetic moneybags who haven't even paid me fully yet!' I said.

'How dare you! *We* gave you the break, *we* cast you, *we* introduced you to Bollywood...' yelled Nimika, and stormed off towards Harry and Bawa.

'You did me no big favours! You needed a great actor at a small price! Buzz off, Nimika! Go complain to your big daddies for all I care!' I shouted after her.

Bawa and Harry began walking towards me.

'You are so different from other heroes, Vishy,' encouraged one anchor. 'Normally, all stars are so boringly diplomatic, but you have the guts to call a spade a spade.'

'Yeah, I am no pushover,' I asserted.

'Are you drunk?' another anchor wanted to know.

'Only on compliments!' I joked as I continued my tirade. 'As I was saying, I came into movies because I love the public, not for money and fame. They need not pay me the balance amount. Entertainment is social service. Movies make people forget their hard lives for a while. Film stars are like social service workers. Money is not everything. Public happiness and satisfaction is paramount. Bringing a smile to a sad face is the only success I desire! I am already getting sick and tired of Train Ticket Films. Too bad I have signed a contract with them for two more movies, though...'

Harry and Bawa had reached me by then.

'Listen, Vishy, this is not helping our movie, enough is enough!' said Bawa, trying to pull me away.

'Don't you dare touch me!' I snapped. 'Harry, get this guy off my back or he will be riding on a stretcher soon!' (Bawa was anyway a tiny man who could've been vaporized with just one proverbial phook; so Harry quickly shielded Bawa behind his huge frame.)

'Cool down, Vishy. Let's watch the premiere. The guests are waiting. You have had your say,' Harry reasoned coolly, whisking me away, and turning to the media, 'we at Train Ticket Films believe in freedom of speech and expression, and Vishy is a good friend who is allowed to badmouth us anytime... Enjoy the movie, folks! It is showtime!'

I walked into the theatre as the flashlights kept clicking with epileptic vigour.

I was already a hero in the eyes of the media. I had taken on the big bosses. I had praised the underdogs, the guys behind the camera and the technicians who never get their due. I could see many anchors smiling at me appreciatively. I had exuded principles, strength, honesty and integrity. How very wrong they all were about my personality profile!

ॐ

'So how was the premiere?' asked Usha as I surfed TV channels to monitor the coverage of our argument.

'Great! They were all in splits and pretty emotional about it. The media loved it!' I exulted.

'Hey,' said Usha, her eyes glued to the telly, 'you and Nimika had a tiff?'

'Yup, Q2,' I said. 'She was saying they are the ones who gave me a break...'

'Hey, are you crazy, Vishy?' shouted Usha, as I kept analysing the channels' views on our tiff. 'This is bad PR! You are even badmouthing Harry and Bawa!'

'So what? I am a man of principles,' I said.

Usha threw me a quizzical look. Perhaps she was thinking: 'That's news to me! You have as many principles as bimbos have grey cells.'

'Tell me how I look,' I said.

'You look dapper, but what has come over you? You have begun making enemies within your own camp,' she sounded worried.

'Yeah, I am speaking my heart out.'

'Balls! You are speaking as if you have lost your mind...'

'But see, all the channels are playing our sound bytes over and over again...see what the anchors are saying...some are praising me to the high heavens for my candour...some are saying producers short-change wannabes anyway...see how much media attention we are getting...'

'So? This is negative publicity.'

'Usha, grow up, how you get noticed doesn't matter. The ends justify the means.'

'And you were just now saying you have principles...'

'Yeah, my principle is: succeed at all costs, and do it fast.'

'The media seems to be on your side, though. They are calling you the underdog, the fresh new voice of truth... you sure have swung opinion in your favour.'

'That was the general idea, baby!'

'You did this spontaneously or...?'

'Arre, how does it matter? Now I ride the sympathy wave. Everyone gets curious about the movie. Have you ever heard of a hero fighting with his heroine, producer and director at a premiere? It has never happened before. And in contrast, the movie has a funny feel-good factor... of course, I wasn't spontaneous...'

'You mean all this was stage-managed?'

'Yeah, by Harry and Bawa.'

'They asked you to badmouth them?'

'Of course, you think I am crazy to take them on?'

'How devious you people are, Vishy!'

'Q2, this is the era of competition. Everyone is trying to get ahead. If you wish to overtake your contemporaries, you need to be smart, bold, controversial and manipulative and—'

'What other cunning plans do they have up their sleeve?'

'Well, keep it to yourself. There will be a major public patch-up on that reality show on Era One...it's called *Yeh Dosti*...you seen it? They put estranged lovers and friends together for a while and ask them to sort out their issues in public...'

'I don't watch such stupid shows.'

'Cool, we will be on it soon.'

'I am not going to be on it.'

'Arre, by *we,* I mean the team at Train Ticket Films...'

♪

Ten days later, we gathered at Bawa's posh flat in Bandra for a secret meeting.

'Wow, Vishy!' said Bawa, handing me a glass of Cointreau liqueur. 'Fantastic news! Great opening! Our movie's a big hit! We have grossed 31 crore in the first week itself!'

'Yeah, and the trade guides are saying it is the dark horse of the year...unexpected success story...' gloated Harry.

'The best part is, it is doing well across all centres, be it A, B or C,' Nimika chipped in.

'That's super! It's all because of your efforts!' I said.

'Hey, you are the secret of our success...our good-luck charm!' said Bawa.

'Listen, Bawa, let's announce our next movie...I have a script that can be shot in under two months...let's ride the wave...' said Harry excitedly.

'Make hay while the sun shines!' grinned Nimika.

'You are the cliché queen, Nimika,' said Bawa.

'So, Vishy, you up to it? Should we begin shooting in a week again?'

'What's the title? And story?' I asked.

'I think we will call it *Hasna Mana Hai.* It's the story of how a village bumpkin becomes an MLA and then the chief minister. It's a bit of a socio-political satire!' said Harry.

'Sounds good to me,' I said. 'We could call it *Beta, Yeh Hai Neta!*'

'Super title, Vishy,' said Bawa. 'By the way, we are giving you a bonus of 75 lakh for the first movie. And a signing amount of 1 crore for the next. Happy?'

'Oh wow, that's really generous! You guys are my godfathers. Whatever you decide!'

'What about the TV show, *Yeh Dosti*? We have to shoot for it next week. Let's discuss that first, we have to stage-manage it perfectly,' reminded Harry.

'Won't the public see through our charade?' Nimika wondered.

'Not at all,' said Bawa. 'They can only suspect, just like a section of the media does. But the public is an ass. Our patch-up will seem engineered, yes, but Indians are too emotional to think logically.'

'Absolutely!' I agreed. 'Let's title our next movie *Public Toh Paagal Hai*.'

We all laughed at that, clinked our glasses, made more don't-tell-anyone plans, and cackled tipsily towards our nth refills.

ૐ

I even won the best male newcomer award for *Paisa To Gul Total Cool*—at a film awards night some two months later.

I gave a resounding speech brimming with the mandatory punchlines and the never-really-meant thanks to family, friends and colleagues, etc.

Later, at the post-awards party at the Marriott, many felt that I could have got the best actor award. But I also learnt that some desperate actors and actresses specialized in getting these much-coveted awards by sleeping with half the jury or by agreeing to do dance routines at such awards functions, or both. Many said the newcomer awards were the only ones that were genuine because (a) you didn't have too many newcomers and, (b) you couldn't fudge the results since the audience clearly knew who was better in his or her first movie.

I was told that all film awards are rigged anyway, and the surprise expressed by the winners is totally stage-managed.

But then, everything about the film industry is phony. The smiles, the hellos, the handshakes, the camaraderie, the rivalry, the chivalry, the bonhomie, the talk, the appreciation—you name it, nothing is genuine.

Anyway, after that night, I never took award functions seriously. Not that I won a single award after that night, either. So now you know why I am a one-award wonder—because I wasn't getting into bed with the jury for cheap thrills.

I even gave an interview eight months later, saying 'more awards are fixed than cricket matches,' and that stirred up quite a controversy. But nobody could ignore me or stop me from bagging good movies, because the audience liked me a lot. Bless the janata's souls.

LEVEL 17

The Party

Fear makes you sleepless—till you
sleep your way to safety.

This was one party Usha couldn't avoid. We were celebrating the stupendous success of our second movie. Yeah, it was the title I had suggested: *Beta, Yeh Hai Neta*. Again, a super-duper hit.

I was on song. I was feeling on top of the world. I had climbed the celluloid ladder at breakneck speed in the short span of just under a year. I was planning to juggle two or three movies at the same time; I was a man in a hurry who wanted to make it big in a jiffy. Bawa had been kind enough to cancel the binding clause in my contract since I had made him quite rich by now.

I was God's blue-eyed boy. Bollywood had reserved a few red carpets for me. The public loved me. The critics loved me. The heavens loved me. Ah, even I loved myself now.

Harry and Bawa had insisted that Usha accompany me since the media was spinning stories that all wasn't fine with our live-in arrangement. I had asked Usha to be diplomatically guarded. She would usually shoot from the hip and shock everyone with her honesty and frankness— that is just not recommended at filmy parties. So, she was to just smile and drink cognac, and Harry said she should mingle around with the journos and make polite conversation.

Filmy parties are like shoots, though. Everyone is usually acting and posturing, and mouthing 'haanji', 'sirjee' and other such sycophantic ego-boosters.

Nimika was cosying up to a Bollywood badshah, a roly-poly financier actually, who was going to partly fund our third project. I wondered if she was sleeping with him—it certainly seemed so, considering that the jewellery-drenched businessman had his arm wrapped around her bare waist. I didn't need to suck up to anyone like this, though, as I was getting lots of offers from the bigger production houses.

Nimika wasn't getting as much footage and as many rave reviews as me, and though she was not saying so openly, pretending graciousness and all that, I got the feeling every now and then that she was pretty cheesed off with me being the media's darling.

'I want to go home,' Usha whispered into my ear as I was digging into the hara bhara kebab.

'Don't be silly, Q2, the party has just begun,' I whispered back.

'Aaah, so the ice maiden is getting tired of our pompous company already,' interrupted Harnoor, a yesteryear actress. Harnoor had done many movies in the late 1980s and early 1990s but remained typecast as a poster girl and starlet, despite having featured with the leading heroes of those days. She had become a friend of mine because I liked to be friends with those who had the right media contacts. Harnoor's cousin was an editor with a film magazine, her friends and acquaintances were head honchos at TV channels and she had a pad in Bandra, where I chilled out alone with her on many evenings.

'No, Harnoor, had a rather tiring day yesterday, you know, at call centres we have to work late into the nights...I have had very little sleep...' said Usha. (Total bunkum. Yesterday had been Usha's day off and she'd just lazed around at home and slept like Rip Van Winkle.)

'Yeah, yeah, you do look a bit tired, don't worry, we will relax in the lounge room,' said Harnoor, carting Usha away, and turning to me, 'and Vishy, Nakul will come to interview you—he's doing a piece for his mag, he's my chela, so don't disappoint him.'

'I won't dare to disappoint you, Harnoorji,' I said, smiling.

As if on cue, someone paraglided into the scene, literally jumped on me, and pumped my extended hand as I struggled to release it from his clammy palm. Nervous nut! But I had to humour him since Harnoor had asked me to.

'Mr Vishnu Shankar! What a pleasure! I am a cub reporter with *Bollywood Bytes*. Could I please interview you? My good name, Nakul,' said this owl-eyed teenager.

Thankfully, Bawa came to my rescue.

'Excuse me, young man,' he said to Nakul, 'do I have your permission to discuss some very urgent business with Vishy?'

'Sure Sir! Bawa sir! What a pleasure! Next month, we are running a super supplement on producers and directors, and all the troubles and travails they have to go through before they hit pay dirt in Bollywood, and Bawa sir, I'd be much obliged and eternally indebted to you if you could...'

'Okay, okay, catch you later,' said Bawa, and we walked away.

'Phew, thanks!' I breathed.

'God has gifted him unlimited talktime for this lifetime,' said Bawa. 'But we could have got a senior journo from *Bollywood Bytes* to interview you. Why this tyro?'

'Harnoor,' I explained curtly.

'Oh. But be careful of her. Most days she is so horny that you will end up getting pregnant,' laughed Bawa.

'C'mon, I have a GF whom I am loyal to. You know that,' I dismissed.

'Yeah, and Harnoor loves to make out with GF-loyalists. Anyway, we are going to announce our third movie now,' said Bawa.

'Now?' I was taken aback.

'You got any probs with that?' asked Bawa.

'No, but I thought we were planning it later,' I said.

'Yeah, slight change of...do you see that businessman with Nimika?' Bawa chin-pointed into the distance.

'Sure...he's been pawing her for quite a while now,' I replied.

'That's Mr Moneybags. For the small price of supplying him with a few starlets, I am getting him to fund 80 per cent of our next project. This is how it works, Vishy. Don't bet your own money. We have the money, yes, but why should we risk it all? Let Mr Moneybags pump in the money after he pumps a few girls...' said Bawa.

'Nimika too?' I wondered.

'Of course. She's our business partner, man, not life partner. She's been on more casting couches that you can count, buddy. How do you think she was bagging all the juicy television commercials? Everyone knows that the brand managers will cast only someone who's ready to warm their beds. Of course, the MBA kinds in advertising and marketing do it classily and all, so I guess the models enjoy being wooed and bedded,' winked Bawa.

'And I thought Bollywood had a patent on the casting couch,' I laughed.

'Well, it is all a give-and-take relationship, my friend. You know how Nimika joined us? Luckily for her, her childless aunt died and left her a small inheritance of about three crore. That is when we became partners, about two years ago, when she invested a part of it in Train Ticket Films. But when she was a struggler, Nimika slept around with more men than a porn star. She won't exactly be losing her virginity to Mr Moneybags... C'mon, don't look so shocked,' said Bawa.

'No, no, I was just thinking of something...' I lied.

'Producers have to pimp around for financiers. This is how it goes. And you know, some wannabes got their first break after a foursome with Harnoor and her editor cousin, Shweta, and...'

'Really? Now I am really shocked!'

'Yeah, you are lucky, Vishy. You made it without becoming a gigolo, but you are an honourable exception in Bollywood.'

I gulped my drink.

'Let's go join the action,' said Bawa as Harry began an announcement.

'Ladies and gentlemen,' said Harry as if he was commentating on a WWE prize fight, 'may I have your attention please! I now present our best project till date! Train Ticket Films thanks you all for making our victory celebration a grand success; and now let me tell you that our third movie, *Campus Cola*, will be the *biggest* and *grandest* of all...'

৵

'There's a call for you,' said Usha, handing me the cordless.

'Hello?'

'Hello, Vishy baba, how ijj you?' said a rustic voice that was obviously not comfortable with the Queen's English.

'Fine, may I know who this is?'

'Good party huhn, yesterday?'

'Arre, who are you?'

'Myjelf Javas Bhola. Speaking from Hamari Dharti Party.'

'Okay...'

'Do something for our party aljo, na.'

'What do you mean?'

'Give uj some donayjun... We give you protecjun phrom bad-bad people...'

'What nonsense is this!'

'Arre, baba, we giving protecjun from underworld. You chaapoing zo much money in Mumbai... Now you giving something to Mumbai back, no...? Givuj ten peti, we don't ask bahut zyada.'

'Go threaten somebody else, Javas, stand outside Churchgate station with a begging bowl in hand!'

'*Theek hai, baba. Ab tu toh gaya...khallaas!*'

'Abbe, chutiye, I have seen many like you, fuck you!'

I hung up angrily while Usha laughed.

'What? Harry doing a telephonic role-play with you again for the next movie? Good dialogues... I suspected that he was calling, nice change of voice he did...' said Usha.

'Q2, don't talk nonsense, that wasn't Harry. It was some party worker from Hamari Dharti Party...he was demanding extortion money...' I said worriedly, wondering if I had made a big mistake by abusing him.

'Stop joking, Vishy!'

'Nope, I swear on us, I am not...'

'Shit! You really abused someone from HDP? Idiot! Don't you know that HDP is one of the most powerful parties? Why couldn't you have handled him more diplomatically? They even have contacts in the underworld!'

'Funny that you are talking about diplomacy! Devil quoting scriptures, huhn?'

'Stop ribbing me. At least you could have spoken politely...'

'Yeah? Politeness is considered a weakness by these idiots. Once you pay, then you have got to keep paying them regularly. Like some bloody monthly salary...'

'This is not good, Vishy. We have just begun our lives here and you are taking on powerful people!'

'Listen, I am not some bloody wimp, I care two hoots, what can they do?'

'Okay, let's at least complain to the cops.'

'Forget it. Let's see what happens.'

'I am scared, Vishy, you even drive alone...what if something happens to you?'

'Usha, stop freaking me out, okay? Que sera sera, what will be will be!'

'At least call up Harry and tell him.'

'Arre, what can he do? He must also have received many such calls!'

'No, talk to him. He might guide you properly.'

'Okay.'

I dialled Harry's cell. It was switched off. He must have gone to his Karjat farmhouse with some starlet. Bawa had gone to Bangkok for the weekend, along with Nimika and the financier, so I didn't feel like disturbing him either. I decided to meet my sounding board in the evening: Harnoor.

～

'Don't worry, Vishy, these things happen. Of course, during our time, things weren't as violent,' said Harnoor as she poured me some bourbon.

'Usha is getting quite worried! She says HDP is full of history-sheeters and mafia dons,' I explained.

'Oho, I told you, na? I will handle it for you,' said Harnoor, and snuggled up closer to me.

She placed her palm on my thigh, patting it gently. She still looked rather sexy, despite her laugh lines and slight wrinkles that she got Botoxed every now and then.

Then she played some Sufi music and we sat in silence for a while. The music was soothing, as was Harnoor's confident demeanour.

'I have a slight backache. You massage my back, and I will get Javas off yours,' she teased.

'C'mon, Harnoorji...you are teasing me...'

'Am I?'

'You know him?'

'Forget all that. Come,' she said, pulling me into her bedroom.

I wondered if 'come' was a loaded pun. Anyway, I pleasured her a bit with a balm-rub and she moaned a lot. Satisfied, she dialled a number after a while. She winked at me and punched the speaker button when a distant phone began ringing.

'Hello, Javasji, what is this I am hearing?'

'Hello Harnoorji! How ijj you? What you saying me?'

'Arre, don't act so innocent, mister. Why did you trouble my chela?'

'Who?'

'Vishy. I've heard you threatened him?'

'Oho, Harnoorji, I asking only for little bit donayjun...'

'Okay. You will get just three lakh. Nothing more.'

'No problum. When?'

'Tomorrow evening. Bye.'

'Theek hai!'

And she hung up.

'Wow, Harnoorji, you know him?' I said, impressed.

'Of course, Vishy, contacts are important. And in Mumbai, everything will be okay if you learn to do a bit of mandavli—negotiation plus compromise.'

'Thank you. I was getting so worried! How do I pay him?'

'My assistant will pay him cash. You can reimburse me later. Happy?'

'Of course, Harnoorji, thoroughly delighted and elated!'

'Now make me ecstatic,' she purred. 'Come, undress me...'

'Oh, Harnoorji, c'mon, you know I have a girlfriend.'

'I am doing so much for you, and you can't even do this much for me?' said Harnoor, and pouted angrily.

'No, no, whatever you say,' I said quickly. 'How ungrateful of me! You have made me happy, and it is my bounden duty to make you happy too!'

I was quite worried that giving her the brush-off now would have the HDP hounding me again.

She smiled seductively and said that nobody could touch me in Mumbai if I was willing to 'touch her everywhere'.

So I disrobed her slowly.

She moaned and kissed me deeply. (Herschelle Gibbs would have called it 'playing tonsil hockey.')

When she was wearing nothing but her birthday suit she asked me to give her a full body massage with olive oil.

After ten minutes, she undressed me slowly...

Sage Vatsyayana would have made umpteen additions and amendments to his *Kama Sutra* if he had watched us for the next hour or so.

I must confess that Sufi music and olive oil are powerful aphrodisiacs.

Anyway, I finally lost my virginity; and immediate worries.

LEVEL 18

Patriot Games

Love is 99 per cent possessiveness,
1 per cent helplessness.

I was shooting like crazy for my third movie. Usha was busy trying to become the head of operations at her call centre now, after some head honcho had died suddenly due to stress-induced heart failure. Most days, she was blind to the world around her, and that included me and my dream run in Bollywood.

Mumbai had surely made both of us 'successoholics'. Somehow, here, what you have already achieved pales in comparison to what can be achieved next. Your eyes and mind are always trained on future goals, on distant work peaks to be conquered, and you sacrifice your present pleasures for future victories.

Two people engrossed in their respective careers is an arrangement that functions like a cool domestic lubricant, though. Late nights were the only time when we met and chilled out for a while, either laughing at some SMS joke or watching a bit of TV. There was never much time left to talk about anything, so there weren't any arguments or flashpoints in our life.

We had a live-in maid now, called Mamta, who was distantly related to the live-in maid Nimika had. Mamta was in her late forties and took good care of us and our household. Life can be hell for a working couple if there is nobody to manage domestic chaos. But thanks to Mamta, life was heaven.

My professional life was equally fun-filled, stress-free and resembled a Xerox copy of Paradise.

I was steadily climbing the Bollywood escalator. And since acting seemed to come as naturally as breathing to me, I definitely felt that I was being phenomenally over-paid for doing something so easy, but I didn't tell anyone that, not even Usha. It is not intelligent to not act tired when you return home after a wonderful day/night, or not to feed the media politically-correct bullshit, like 'behind the glamour lies a lot of grit and hard work that's never seen,' and so on.

Everyone hates anybody who makes easy money, so you have to keep complaining and lying about erratic work schedules, early morning shoots, gruelling dubbing routine, incessant nerve-wracking business class travel on domestic and international airlines, screwed-up biological clock, tasteless five-star hotel cuisine...blah blah blah...how tough is your life!

ᠵ

Saturday was Usha's day off and I decided to surprise her by returning early from my shoot. Harry packed up at 6 p.m. and I reached our pad at 8 p.m. What the hell! Ten pairs of footwear were parked outside the door. As I rang the bell I heard huge peals of laughter from within. Definitely Usha entertaining her call centre colleagues! Darn, just when I was thinking of taking her out for a nice, cosy, romantic dinner.

Mamta let me in and whispered, '*Wohi log.*'

'Hey, Vishy!' screamed Naresh, 'welcome, welcome, make yourself at home!'

Everyone laughed, as if he were Russell Peters in his element.

Did I smell some marijuana in the air? Shit! They were smoking dope in my living room! What the hell had come over Usha? Why was she entertaining junkies at our pad? I surveyed the hippie crowd. Nine guys, two girls—and that sex ratio included Usha.

'Hi honey, how come you are back early?' asked Usha.

'Early pack up,' I explained.

'Hey, dude, fix yourself a drink, we are about to play dumb charades, come join us,' said someone.

'No, thanks,' I excused myself. 'I have a splitting headache, plus there's this early morning shoot. You guys chill.'

'C'mon, Vishy, be a sport!' urged Usha.

'Tired...some other time,' I said, walking away.

'Cool, catch you later, when you aren't such a big star anymore,' remarked Usha.

'Keep praying for that to happen,' I said.

I was seething, but what could I do—apart from plugging in my iPod and listening to some heavy metal? I decided to give Usha a piece of my mind once the party ended—then decided to let it pass. I don't know when I dozed off...

'Honey, wake up, you haven't even had dinner,' said Usha, shaking me awake.

'Hmmm...leave me alone,' I protested sleepily.

'You have a fever?' she asked, feeling my forehead and neck.

'No,' I mumbled, wondering if anger was enhancing my body temperature.

'At least join us for dinner, they will all be leaving soon,' she said.

'Not well, Usha, you guys carry on, apologize on my behalf,' I said, putting on my trademark diplomatic tone.

'Okay, I will also eat later then.'

'No, no, you eat...'

'No way! That's the least I can do for you.'

Well, at least she loved me still—unless she was also acting. Anyway, forget it, not worth fighting over it and spoiling the golden mood that had lasted a few months now, I thought.

We grabbed dinner after about an hour.

'You are such a boor, Vishy, they all were saying that you've developed a starry attitude,' said Usha.

'Let them, Q2. They should understand that I really wasn't feeling well.'

'You aren't angry, are you?'

'Not at all. As long as you are happy, I am cool,' I lied.

'I am so lucky to have such an understanding BF,' she smiled.

I wondered if she would give me more time and transform into the kind of devoted wife you get to see in Bollywood movies. Perhaps Usha would metamorphose into a dutiful wife who will believe in karva chauth and worship me as her god. It's time we got married, I thought; solemnizing our relationship might make her less bohemian. Anyway, there was no harm trying.

'Q2, will you marry me?'

'Thought you'd never ask.'

ॐ

We got married a month later in Delhi at a small ceremony at home.

Thankfully, both Usha and I agreed on a small guest list comprising only immediate family and friends.

Usha's dad and my folks got along famously. Since Usha, too, was an only child, I wasn't marrying into a huge family, which I was happy about.

The media got to know about my marriage a week later—so you can imagine how irked the gossip columnists were with us. But Bawa had already chalked out a plan to assuage the collective media angst.

Since my third movie was near completion, and was about to be released a month later, Bawa said that this would be the perfect occasion to host a party for the media and Bollywood moguls at Marriott. And since that made professional sense, I had gone with his idea, though Usha said that it was the last public gathering she was ever going to attend with me. (She stuck to her guns in the coming years, and we were never again seen together at parties or award functions after that day.)

After the grand reception in Mumbai, Usha and I took off on a quiet honeymoon to Sikkim, not some exotic, foreign locale—which decision surprised quite a few.

Usha and I were die-hard Indians who had decided long ago that our holidays would only be spent in India. (We never changed our stance. And it might sound odd to you, but even after becoming a film star, I never liked travelling abroad, and always used to convince my producers and directors to shoot within India's territorial limits. The media even called me 'Swadeshi Star' and 'Xenophobic Vishy', but I took it as a compliment that underscored my fierce sense of patriotism.)

⌇

Campus Cola was a big hit. Harry and Bawa joked that they could now retire since they had made enough money to last a lifetime. Nimika was unhappy though, since the media didn't give her the credit that was due. She was quite miffed that despite having delivered three hit movies as my leading lady, she still wasn't breaking into the big league. Perhaps it was all destiny, I reckoned, but some actors and actresses don't do well even if their movies take the box office by storm. Such examples are legion in Bollywood.

Me, I was on a roll. I was getting offers by the dozen; I was reading ten scripts per week; I was getting deluged with phone calls from the big production houses. Bollywood worships the rising sun, and everyone wants to milk your potential and popularity till your cinematic udders dry up. Meanwhile, Usha was slogging her butt off, since she had recently been promoted to ops head.

After *Campus Cola*, I shifted loyalty from Train Ticket Films to Kabi Mehtai Productions. They were the real big guns. Harry and Bawa were happy for me; they wished me well, saying that we should do something real big together in the coming years. Kabiji gave me a humongous signing amount and we signed a contract for an obscene amount of money. Let me tell you how I got the offer...

༄

I got a call from Atul Mehtai himself. Atul was Kabiji's eldest son and apparent heir to their multi-million-rupee movie production empire. I was over the moon, I had been considered by Kabi Mehtai Productions! The industry acronym for them was KAMP; and everyone said that if you joined them, you were set for life. Every actor and actress belongs to one camp or the other—it's the Bollywood version of the ghetto mentality that ensures survival of the species. When I relayed the news to Harnoor, she said that it was more rewarding to be signed up by Kabiji than to win an award, because just one KAMP film under your belt meant a whopping 100 or 200 per cent jump in your remuneration. KAMP only backed the best actors—so being cast by them also meant that you had picked up an unofficial best actor award. Anyway, let me tell you how the call went; and how I had egg on my face in the end.

'Hi, Mr Vishnu Shankar, this is Atul here...you know, from Kabi Mehtai Productions, perhaps you have heard of us...' said a pansy-like voice, which I didn't trust at all.

I thought someone was playing a prank on me.

C'mon, I was just three movies old. KAMP only signed veterans and the top five heroes and heroines. Even big-shot contemporary stars like Sarwin Narang, Neerav Khanna and Peter Makhani were dying to work with them.

'*Abbe, kyon chutiya bana raha hai, saaley?*' I asked Atul. He was unfazed.

'Okay, my call sounds incredible, I guess. I will text you our official landline number at KAMP, call me in five minutes,' said Atul, hanging up.

'Yeah, yeah, someone thinks I am still a gullible kid eating Cerelac and watching Cartoon Network...' I mumbled to myself.

Anyway, my cell flashed a text after a minute.

Welcome aboard KAMP, Mr Vishnu Shankar, thinking of casting you as main lead in our forthcoming comedy film, *Sach Na Bola Karo Yaaron*. Pls call on any of the following numbers to get in touch with Atul Mehtai—Roshana Barucha, Media Manager, KAMP.

'What the fuck!' I yelled.

I whistled shrilly, simulating part horror and part ecstasy. 'So it was indeed Atul? *The* Atul Mehtai of *the* KAMP? Oh, no! Why the hell did you have to abuse him, Vishy?' I rebuked myself.

I punched in their number. I took a deep breath. A distant phone rang thrice. My heartbeats thumped equally loudly.

'Welcome to KAMP, Mr Vishnu Shankar,' said an anglicized voice.

'Yes, I...would you...' I stuttered, angry with myself for behaving like a complete fool by suspecting a prank.

'Atul Mehtaiji is waiting for your call. Shall I put you through?'

'Sure.'

'And before that, I have a personal request, Mr Shankar,' the lady said.

'Yeah, go ahead.'

'Will you autograph a DVD of your first movie for me? My sister and I are big fans of yours...'

'Hey, my pleasure, Ms...'

'Call me Roshy, all call me that, and one small piece of friendly advice...hmm...' she dropped her voice, and broke off hesitatingly.

'Advice? Go ahead, Roshy, all ears...'

'If Atul wants to meet you alone, then wear casuals—jeans and tees; if both Atul and his dad will be there, dress as if you are about to meet the Queen of England—suit and tie—the old geezer is a bit old-fashioned and eccentric ...' her voice dipped by infinite decibels to become a conspiratorial whisper.

For two minutes more, she continued telling me what to say, what not to say, when to laugh, when not to laugh, etc. She signed off with, '...but don't tell them I told you all this...I am a just big fan of yours, so I did...'

'Thanks, Roshy.'

'Will put you through now, hold on...'

'Mr Vishnu Shankar!' said the same pansy-like voice cheerfully. 'So you see? We aren't playing any pranks on you!'

'Oh no, Sir! Sorry, a few weeks ago...someone, Sir, pretended to be a Hollywood director...I'm so sorry for... for abusing you...'

'Hey, c'mon, I enjoyed it, it was the high point of the day! And call me Atul. Reserve the "sir" for Dad.'

'Okay, Atul! And please call me Vishy!'

'Okay, Vishy, we need your help. You know, we were planning on casting Neerav for our next—that's no secret, but he's acting mighty pricey, demanding an astronomical amount. Imagine, someone asking for ten crore! Don't you think that's idiotic?'

'Well, I can't comment on the remuneration demands of my senior colleagues, but as for me, I think I am more reasonable in my expectations.'

'Good answer. Very diplomatic. You have said his demand is not reasonable, that he is a greedy pig, and that you are the flavour of the season in the same breath.'

'You speak so well...you remind me of an old friend...'

'Okay, thanks for the compliment. We will pay you three crore. A fifty-lakh bonus if the movie is a hit, at our discretion. But we want bulk dates for two months. If this is acceptable...'

'Atul, I am dying to do a KAMP movie! I don't want to bullshit you. This is my biggest break. I need you guys, man, you don't need me at all! I am ready to do it for even half of what you are offering!'

'Your honesty is much appreciated. But now listen. We at KAMP never short-change anyone...'

'Absolutely, Atulji. Whatever you say!'

'Now, if you are free this evening, Dad would like to meet you personally.'

'Dad? You mean Kabiji wants to meet me? This is...I... wow...this is indeed an honour...I thought he never met minor actors like me...'

'He likes you, Vishy. And the sky's the limit if this liking grows over the years...'

'Thanks, Atul, what time?'

'Be at our Juhu bungalow, at 7 p.m. sharp. Dinner at 9 p.m. You know where it is?'

'Who doesn't? It's a landmark in Mumbai.'

'But I must warn you. You'll have to tolerate Dad's stories. I am not invited for the meeting, so we will meet later this week. And yes, Vishy, one more thing...don't get any gifts or bouquets or anything for Dad. That's the only thing he hates—people thinking they can give him anything he can't buy himself.'

'Yeah, got it, I'll be there!'

'And don't be too servile with Dad! Be diplomatic, yes, but speak your mind! Dad hates hypocrites, too!'

'Will keep that in mind, Atul. Thanks for the tips.'

'Okay, thanks for calling, Vishy, all the best! Bye!'

ॐ

The liveried servant led me into Kabiji's study. He pushed open the door without knocking, ushered me in and left. It was as if I had stepped into a huge library. The walls were lined with stacks of books nestling in mahogany bookshelves. Kabiji was seated with his back to the door, perhaps immersed in some tome. Cigar smoke filled the air. Havana? Maybe.

'Sir, good evening, Sir!' I said from the doorway. 'May I come in?'

'Welcome, welcome, Vishy! My pleasure to meet a superstar! Thanks for accepting my invitation,' he said, swivelling around and rising from the heavy leather chair.

'Thank you for considering me for your movie, Sir!'

'What books do you usually read? I am reading *The God Delusion* now.'

'Huh? I...I am sorry, Sir, I don't read too many books. I have never been much of a reader...'

'Good. Honest. Never be sorry for the way you are, Vishy. Sit down wherever... Me, I am a bookworm. But that's my problem, right?'

'Why should it be a problem, Sir? If reading books is your idea of fun, then it is good, Sir!'

'And why is it good?'

'Well...you can be happy all alone...you won't need anyone...needing people is the real problem, Sir...and you are lucky that you can keep yourself entertained easily anytime...so it is good.'

'And what is your idea of fun?'

'Sir, I like to go on long drives with my wife, walk along the beach, play with my gadgets and gizmos, watch movies...'

'What drives you?'

'Well, I guess the desire to show my father that I have made it!'

'Because?'

'Because throughout my teenage years I was a loser, Sir. An academic failure.'

'So they gave you an inferiority complex?'

'You bet, Sir!'

'Drink? Smoke? Sorry I got carried away.'

'Not at all Sir. I wouldn't mind a Bloody Mary, Sir.'

'Nice choice,' he said, and spoke into his intercom. 'Okay, now let's step into my private garden.'

He pressed a button under his table and a huge bookshelf swung on its vertical pivot like a revolving door.

'I call it my secret Shangri-La!' said Kabiji.

'Amazing idea. Just like in old Hindi movies, where smugglers—' I broke off, biting my tongue. What the hell was I saying?

Kabiji laughed loudly.

'Well, Vishy, don't be afraid to speak your mind. Now, let us smuggle you into the garden. Come!' he said cheerily.

ॐ

'Meet my mistress,' Kabiji coolly introduced as we snaked through the bookshelf-cum-revolving door into his private garden, which was shut in like a greenhouse, with lots of creepers shading it from the sun and the public gaze of the terraces and balconies of adjacent bungalows.

A gorgeous babe wearing a tight tank top and a micromini was sitting in a high-value antique chair covered with burgundy antimacassars. She was a study in erotica.

'Hi,' I said to her smiling, 'they call me Vishy.'

'Mizinah,' she said, crossing her legs seductively to reveal more thigh.

Then she got up and sat on Kabiji's lap as he sank into a huge lounge chair.

'Well, she's my laptop model,' he said, fondling her waist. 'I am fifty-three. She is twenty. Old men should sleep with young women to feel youthful and buoyant. This was the brilliant advice sages gave to kings of yore.'

I marvelled at his candour. Only the phenomenally rich or the breathtakingly poor don't care a damn for what the world thinks about them. The financial polar opposites on the ladder of material evolution are the only ones that have shown their collective middle fingers to the world.

'You know, Mizinah,' said Kabiji, kissing her on the lips, 'Vishy abused Atul today.' He broke into raucous laughter as he stroked her thigh and winked at me.

'Oh, sorry about that, Sir...total...disastrous misunderstanding... I...I thought someone was playing the fool...'

'Not at all, every now and then Atul should get a good dose of foul words from someone, otherwise our money and position will go to his head... I will give you one lakh rupees for every abuse you hurl at him from now on...' laughed Kabiji. 'You can make more money giving him gaalis than by acting in these roles that will only get you a few taalis.'

'Nice rhyme, Sirji, you are a born poet,' I said sycophantically, and laughed deliberately, while Mizinah rolled her eyes in boredom. Perhaps she'd heard that line a million times.

'Okay, let's get down to brass tacks,' Kabiji said.

'Sure, Sir!'

'I want you to do this film with Mizinah. You like her?'

'Of course, Sir, yes, she...she is good, Sir...'

'C'mon, talk like a man. What do you like about her?'

'Sir?'

'You heard me. Stop stalling for time. Describe what you like about her.'

Mizinah glanced at me seductively/invitingly/piercingly.

'Sir...Sir...this is so...'

'Embarrassing?'

'Yes, Sir, you hit the nail on the head...'

'Young man, how will you become a great actor if you are so inhibited? Don't you know that the first step towards stardom is to lose all your inhibitions?'

'Yes, you are right, Sir!'

'I *know* I am right, I don't need your affirmation of what I already know about myself.'

'Oh, sorry, Sir...'

'Okay, I am waiting, and I haven't got all day. Your time starts now. Mizinah is dash-dash-dash... Fill in the blanks, please.'

'She is...is...ravishing...ummm...'

'And?'

'Stunningly beautiful...'

'And?'

'...desirable...'

'And? Okay, get up, Mizinah, and turn around,' he ordered.

Mizinah got up and twirled around a bit.

'She's a sex goddess, Sir!' I exclaimed.

'Exactly! Now you have hit the bullseye!'

'Thank you, Sir!'

'Okay, Mizinah, go prepare the Jacuzzi,' he commanded.

Mizinah smiled at me and left the scene.

'A Jacuzzi is so relaxing, Vishy. Ever tried it?'

'No, Sir.'

'Today's your lucky day.'

'And Mizinah,' he shouted after her, 'Vishy will join you soon. But no hanky-panky, okay? I am your only god!'

She turned and blew a flying kiss. I didn't know if it was directed at him or me—probably both.

Mizinah returned after ten minutes as I was sipping my second Bloody Mary. Kabiji was nursing a screwdriver. He mixed the drinks himself. Mizinah sank into her chair and he served her some bluish-purple cocktail.

I was getting turned on just by looking at her. I had never seen anyone so very desirable at such close quarters. It was as if she had been carved out of the rarest of Carrara marble and brought to life to make men grovel at her feet, asking her to at least *look* at them. She was more gorgeous than any Miss World or Miss Universe or any beauty queen I had ever seen. Where could she be from? Lebanon? Peshawar? Iran? Definitely not Indian. I tried to be casual and cool. I don't think I succeeded.

'Now, stand with your back towards him, and remove your skirt,' ordered Kabiji suddenly.

She dropped her skirt.

I gulped. I could have jumped on her, I was feeling so horny.

'Now, slowly, really slowly, remove your top...okay Vishy, describe her bottom.'

I was in sheer agony under my zipper.

'...breathtaking...amazingly sculpted...a work of art...'

She removed her top. She wasn't wearing a bra.

'What do you have to say about her bare back?'

'Lovely, flawless skin...deliciously curvaceous...totally dhamaal...'

'Now you are talking! Do you want her to drop her panties, too?'

'Oh...no...Sir...'

'So you aren't attracted to her?'

'No, Sir, I mean...yes, Sir...I am...but I am married...'

'So am I, Vishy, but am I committing a crime by appreciating beauty and taking beauty to bed? Isn't rejecting beauty a far greater crime than accepting your natural attraction for it? Am I being unnatural?'

'Not at all, Sir.'

'Okay, Mizinah, show us all you've got!'

She slowly slid down the last piece of black velvet covering her bottom. A gorgeous human sculpture indeed! Then my entire body became stiff as she slowly turned to face me. She stood there tantalizingly. All she was wearing was a smile.

What a beauty! 37-27-36!

'So Vishy, now you can continue your drinks with Mizinah in the Jacuzzi. And don't return till you guys have developed some chemistry. But no touching her now! That will happen only in the movie!' commanded Kabiji.

A naked Mizinah led a fully-clothed me into a Jacuzzi in the centre of a huge hall that had marble flooring and walls covered with teak.

She asked me to doff my suit, shirt and all else. I did as directed.

We lay down in the swirling, warm, soothing, bubbling water for about twenty minutes.

We didn't touch each other. We didn't speak. I just kept looking at her. She kept smiling at me.

Then she stepped out, and playfully pulled me out too. She passed me a bathrobe and slipped into extremely erotic red lingerie.

You have heard of casting couches. This was some kind of casting Jacuzzi.

We got dressed and returned to Kabiji in the garden. Well, at least I got dressed, but the only thing Mizinah wore, apart from the lingerie, was some mascara and lipstick.

'So how was the experience, Vishy?' he asked.

'Well…Sir…soothing…relaxing…exhilarating…'

'Ecstasy, my friend, it was pure ecstasy for you, right?'

'Absolutely, Sir!'

'Okay, this is your contract. Read it and sign it.'

'No, Sir, I am going to sign it without reading. I trust you.'

'Good. You understand that I have so much that I don't need to steal anything from anyone.'

'Yes, Sir.'

'Would you like Mizinah to give you a full body massage?'

'Uh? No, thank you, Sir.'

'You are afraid that you will get aroused, right?'

'Exactly, and you said no touching...'

'I was joking, my friend, I usually joke and tease raw virgins like you.'

'Sir, I am not a virgin...'

'Anyone who hasn't slept with Mizinah is a virgin. You don't know what all she can do. You will discover pleasure points in your body that you never thought existed. Vishy, unless you sleep with your leading lady, you will never be able to get the right emotions. Okay, not tonight, but one of these days, I am going to watch you and Mizinah make love. That is my only hobby. To see youngsters understanding each other. Agreed?'

'Whatever you say, Sir.'

'Good. Let us have a few more rounds of drinks, then we will head for dinner. You are veg or non-veg?'

'Pure veg.'

'What a pity! No animal instincts then. My friend, unless you eat non-veg, you will never get the raw energy to zoom ahead of the rest of the pack. Sarwin, Neerav and Peter are all non-veg. Veg food doesn't help develop the killer instinct.'

'My raw ambitions and unpleasant memories of a troubled youth fill me with enough energy, Sir. With your help, I can make it real big, irrespective of what I eat.'

'Hmm...spoken like a winner...okay, now let me go get a quickie. We'll be right back. Enjoy your drinks, while I enjoy her,' he said, squeezing Mizinah's bottom, and they disappeared into another room.

I waited for fifteen minutes. Surprisingly, I wasn't feeling guilty about the naked romp with Mizinah. It was so pure and natural and innocent and...yes, divine! I was feeling happy.

They returned, satisfied. We headed for dinner after an hour. Kabiji kept talking about how he had made it big in Bollywood, about casting couches and mistresses of famous stars, about loan sharks and underworld financiers, about his contacts in the income tax department, about how he chose scripts and the cast, about how to stay ahead of the game by changing the rules of the game every so often, about how he collected Renaissance art...

Yes, Atul had warned me about it all, but I was really enjoying Kabiji's monologue. Here was a sincere, well-read, well-travelled, classy, truthful, straight, non-hypocritical person who made no bones about the fact that he was a simple human with simple desires. Suddenly, I wanted to be just like him. Perhaps I would...

Mizinah kissed me on my cheeks as I bade them goodbye at the driveway at 9.30 p.m. Pure heaven.

ॐ

Well, to give you a fair idea of how much I was worth now, I could book a posh apartment in Bandra. Usha and I moved into our new home a month after I signed up with KAMP.

Those days, I used to think of Jana, and convince myself that the loser was dead wrong about life.

If you ask me, intelligence is all about being adaptive. It is sheer folly to be an idealistic philosopher. And, by the way, even making money is a kind of philosophy with some. The word 'philosophy' means love of knowledge or knowing. And what would you call a person who loves knowing the taste of riches and fame? A philosopher. And how can you know what it feels like to be wealthy if you live like a poor beggar?

I felt like calling up Jana and shattering his theories but fought the temptation, since I had decided not to argue with him any further on any subject. I don't know why I kept thinking of him. Perhaps, somewhere deep down, I felt the need to be a bit like him? Or perhaps, I was one of those pseudo-intellectuals who felt happy if someone of above-average intelligence provided them some conversational time? Or perhaps, I was always looking for an evolved father figure since Dad had not deemed it fit to ever have a mature conversation with me?

Anyway, damn it all. As Kabiji had said, not wanting anything is happiness. I decided not to want Jana at all.

It's not possible to not want Jana, said something from within me.

The King and I

Flaunting one's success is more
pleasurable than success itself.

I had called up Arpita many months ago to get my mind off pansy-type, super-snoopy gossip columnists. 'All these nosey parkers should be hung on a thorny clothesline—*after* sending them on a joyride in a washing machine...the bastards have so much keeda in them...' I had once whinged to her. I was cheesed off because some papers carried Page 3 speculative news items titled 'Mizinah's Lovers?'; 'Wet, Wild Wednesday'; 'Viagra Moments'; and the likes. The noontime tabloids had even printed intimate photographs of Kabiji, Atul, me and Mizinah at a private poolside party in Khandala. Usha had been pretty miffed with me, and I wanted to give a supari for the paparazzi who had leaked the pics. Talking again to Arpita would be a bit of a stress buster, and also take me back to my erstwhile uncomplicated life in Pune. Somehow, one never forgets one's roots. We usually leave our hearts and our purity of thoughts somewhere out there, don't we?

'Hey, Arpi, kemcho?' I had trilled.

'Hey, Vishy dear! How are you, man? Wrong question. You are all over the gossip mags and the newspapers!' she had cooed.

'Well, life has been kind.'

'Nice, and as we predicted, you have coolly forgotten us—'

'Oh, c'mon Arpi, you are my lifeline, only I have been so busy that... By the way, how's Jana?'

'Well...what can I say, Vishy? He quit Cosmos a long time ago and is back at the ghat, I guess—'

'What! I can't believe it! I thought we had brought that guy's life back on track!'

'Well, Vishy, perhaps that's his calling: to live like a vagabond—'

'Why did you let him do something so stupid again? Why didn't you talk him out of it?'

'Vishy, we aren't on talking terms. He walked out on me one evening, and whenever I try to talk to him at the ghat, he just walks away. He's in pretty bad shape, too.'

'Oh, I am so sorry to hear that. Listen Arpi, I feel like driving down in the night, would it be okay if I come in sometime late? You know, avoid the crowd kind of thing, and vanish early?'

'Hey, sure, would be great to see you, when will you come?'

'Hmmm...it's nine now...I will leave by ten or eleven... guess I'll make it by one or two tonight, is that cool?'

'Of course, Vishy, super! Will be waiting for you!'

'Ciao, buddy, catch you in your nightie then—'

'Don't forget to bring along your seductive charm then—'

'I won't. Bye!'

⤳

I had zipped across in my Audi, thanks to the Mumbai–Pune expressway, in two and a half hours flat. By the time I reached Arpita's flat, it was nearly 2 a.m.

'Vishy! Oh, Vishy!' she said, giving me a tight bear hug. 'How very handsome you look! Hmmm…smelling nice too… sexy cologne…Burberry?'

'No, Azzaro.'

'Lovely! It feels so good to see you!'

'Ditto. To tell you the truth, I came to see Jana, too.'

'Yeah, I guessed as much. You've always had a soft corner for him. Guess he must be at the ghat.'

'Cool, mind if I check him out?'

'Not at all, I'd like to come too, but he doesn't like me anymore—'

'Why, what happened? Any argument?'

'Well, you know how he is, always philosophical and never practical. I tried dinning some sense into him, and he quietly left our pad one evening. He hasn't returned ever since. And he doesn't talk to me when I try to—'

'Okay…I'm dying to meet him, though. Should I come back or would you have hit the sack? I'd like to drive back before the world wakes up.'

'Arre, we will have an early morning coffee or something at Blue D, go talk to him and come back.'

'Done.'

When I reached the ghat, I saw that the gazebo housed more people now. The colony crowd called them bhatakti atmas, but then, aren't we all? Do any of us really know what we are doing on Planet Earth, why we are here, from where we have come and where we will go?

I saw someone sitting at the park bench, staring at the river. Long kurta. Flowing mane. Definitely Jana.

I stood behind him quietly. He didn't notice my arrival.

Our conversations didn't require the usual preambles, like 'hi' and 'hello' anyway. We could take up the thread precisely from where we had left off.

'Why don't you do something, Jana, other than staring at rivers?' I asked.

'Being is more important than doing,' he said, without turning back.

'Being what? Being a lazy bum?'

'That's the point, Vishy. Just being. Not being something or somebody. Not being encompassed by definitions of either active or lazy.'

'All this is philosophical bullshit, Jana. You aren't going to get anything out of it.'

'Listen, Vishy, life is not about getting anything or going anywhere. Life is relaxation.'

'Just another name for pure laziness.'

'So what's wrong with that? Even if I accept your terminology, lazy people are the most harmless. You won't find a lazy man raping or murdering or robbing anyone. He is in a state of masterly inactivity, and thus he discovers his true self—'

'And the true self is lazy? What nonsense! The universe is full of energy and is always dynamic—'

'Vishy, you are missing the point entirely. Energy is like a river, agreed, and it's always flowing, just like life. But workaholics don't flow with the stream; they fight it. Life is already in motion. So you can afford to be still. Life is like a train, and you don't run inside a train compartment to reach your destination faster, do you? You don't control the engine from the passenger seat.'

'You are incorrigible, Jana. I can't change you.'

'And why would you want anyone to change? That's a pathological and psychological disease. Let a rose be a rose. If you won't get offended, may I say something?'

'Sure, go ahead.'

'Vishy, you aren't intelligent. You might be rich and famous, but your intelligence is close to that of a fourteen-year-old boy. In fact, that's the average intelligence of the entire world—'

'I don't need your certificates; I know I am intelligent—'

'You fail yourself. Intelligence never knows. Intelligence is realizing that one can never know anything; that one will always be in awe of this mysterious existence eternally!'

'Balls to all this talk, Jana. One day you will not have enough money to feed yourself and you will come to me, begging.'

'Even if I do that, as you so grandly predict, that will still not make me wrong. Money without wisdom is like a monkey wielding a surgeon's scalpel.'

'Yeah? But it still beats wisdom without money on any given day.'

'Money, success, fame—all these will vanish with you, Vishy.'

'Damn you! You are a coward who took no risks! Look at me! Thousands of fans all over India—and counting. You know, 157,598 people follow me on Twitter—and growing. I have 4,454 friends on Facebook. What do you have? Apart from bullshit talk?'

'Whom are they following, Vishy?'

'Huh?'

'You think they like you? They love you? They respect you?'

'Of course! Any doubts? They worship me wherever I go.'

'Vishy, nobody loves you or respects you. Stop suffering from that delusion. They love and respect your fame and money.'

'Look at you, Jana. Back to square one, living the life of a loser. I have it all, man. Cars, houses, money, servants, fame, everything... What do you have?'

'Myself,' he said laconically.

'I have myself, too.'

'No, you have sold your soul. Don't tell me you did nothing nefarious to get where you have got.'

'Balls! Success came to me on a platter.'

'When God wants to really punish you, He rewards you pretty heavily first.'

'You are an idiot, spinning stupid philosophical theories all the time.'

'Is that why you like talking to me?'

'I don't like talking to losers like you. But I thought I could get some sense into you—'

'Vishy, you are the loser. In the end, when your time on earth is up, you will see where all this takes you—'

'Nonsense. I am fearless. I am not afraid of anything!'

'Then why are you afraid to accept that you are a depraved, corrupt, perverted soul?'

'I am not!'

'You are not what? Not depraved, or not afraid to admit you are depraved?'

'I am not depraved.'

'Says who?'

'Listen, you beggar. I came here to look you up, to help you get a life, to put your life back on track—'

'Vishy, ever heard of a fish rescuing an ocean?' he asked, laughing loudly.

'Don't screw my mind!'

'You don't have one.'

'Jana, enough. I have made it in life. You have fucked up yours.'

'Fine, suit yourself. Anyway, what did you come here for?'

'Uh...well...just to look you up—'

'No, you came to show off your success. But neither your fame nor your celeb status impresses me.'

'Who's trying to impress you, dude? You think I care a rat's ass about your opinion?'

'Then why don't you just leave me alone? I have no time for intellectual pygmies like you.'

'You're a miserable egoist talking about sour grapes, Jana—'

'You know, Vishy, I just hate my intelligence.'

'Yeah? Why?'

'Because it is the only thing that prevents me from enjoying your wonderful company.'

'Fuck you, Jana!'

'That's becoming your trademark parting words.'

I left him there at 3 a.m. Alone and lost to the real world at the Burning Ghat.

But he looked so damn tranquil and peaceful.

Did he really mean that he wasn't bothered by my success? Wasn't he feeling any envy? Perhaps he was just acting. No, he was a bad actor. What the hell was his trip in life? Balls to him, anyway...

༼

As it always happens with me, I was tiring of my routine and getting bored stiff with all the filmy folk, their fake smiles and pretentious talk. Was I missing Jana and his simplicity? But after our showdown many moons ago, I hadn't got in touch with him. I had called up Arpita and she'd said that Jana had moved out of the ghat, and was untraceable now. In all probability, he had become an itinerant penniless monk travelling somewhere. I was desperate to trace him, and though there was just a one-in-a-billion chance of him responding, I still sent him an email asking him to call me back.

He did call after a week and I was ridiculously joyful on hearing his voice.

'Hey Jana! How are you, dude, and where are you?' I asked.

'Well, still on Planet Earth, I guess,' said Jana.

'Aha, the sense of humour is still intact, good—'

'So what did you mail me for?'

'Hey, listen Jana, I need your help. There's this movie that's happening and the director is totally unable to crack the climax. Plus, the storyline needs some tweaking. I thought you could chip in with your ideas, and I am sure only you can come up with something brilliant, since you are a genius—'

'Cut the crap. I am not into writing bullshit stuff for Hindi films.'

'Jana please, this is damn important for me. Plus, you will get to make some money.'

'Some things never change. When will you realize that I don't do anything for money?'

'Okay, do it for me. Look, I am sorry if I hurt you during our showdown—'

'Don't live in delusions that you are important enough to hurt me. I have never taken you seriously.'

'Cool, accepted that you are the most evolved amongst us and totally immune to us lesser mortals. You are above all of us, and you know it. But I need you on this. It will be fun, Jana, just like old times. Imagine, us sitting and brainstorming and having fun coming up with some groovy ideas—'

'There are enough good scriptwriters in Mumbai, so count me out—'

'Please Jana, I need you!'

'Stop whining! Okay, tell you what, if I feel up to it, I'll buzz you later. Let me sleep over it.'

'C'mon yaar, we need to do this in a month's time... plus...er...I have been missing you, dude.'

'Now who's the beggar? You or me? You have an emotional need for me.'

'Fine. I am the beggar, okay? I am begging you to help me!'

'Fine. It will be fun to help a rich beggar for once.'

'So will you come over?'

'Do you suffer from short-term amnesia, apart from your legendary stupidity? Didn't I just tell you that I'll think about it and let you know?'

'Stop acting pricey, Jana!'

'The man who wants nothing from life can act in any manner he chooses to. Okay, I gotta go now, catch you later—'

'Okay, king, but do call—'

'I will try to, beggar. Bye.'

He had hurt my ego and ridiculed my achievements once again.

Damn! This guy's screwing my mind. He called me a *beggar*? I am a bloody millionaire, dammit! The bloody bastard!

I will fuck his trip so badly that he won't forget me in many lifetimes to come.

Yeah, it will serve him right for saying I am not important enough!

I am the eighth or ninth on the Bollywood ladder and he thinks I am insignificant?

I will show him who I am! What is he so arrogant about?

Let him call. I will seduce him into being a script doctor and hit him below the belt. His intellect will not survive my crooked intelligence. I chalked up a simple plan to get his goat. His mega composure would be broken, and that would delight me no end. I will tell you how I went about my devious plan by and by. Now let's get back to how my life with Usha was shaping up.

꒰ꕤ꒱

'Where were you yesterday evening?' I had asked her sometime back.

'Why?' retorted Usha.

'What do you mean why? Why do you have to answer questions with questions?'

'Hey, I was chilling out with friends.'

'Which friends?'

'Oh my god, now don't tell me you are again suspecting me of disloyalty and keeping tabs on me—'

'Listen, Usha, I am just concerned that you are clubbing with junkies—'

'Don't you dare call them that! And, by the way, everyone can be called a junkie, everyone is addicted to something. You are a success junkie, someone is an adrenaline junkie and someone else is a spiritual junkie—'

'Q2,' I said, trying to soften her up (not that I succeeded in the effort), 'I don't like you going out with Naresh and gang.'

'Stop being so possessive, will you?'

'Love *means* possessiveness!'

'I need my space, Vishy, and I get bored all alone. You are always out shooting, what am I supposed to do? Vegetate at home when not at work?'

'But why don't I hear of any girls in your just-hanging-out-with-my-buddies explanations—'

'I am not giving you any explanation. I owe you none. Now you listen. Do I interfere in your choice of friends? I don't like Nimika one bit, at least not now, I think she's usually giving you the glad eye, but do I ever—'

'Now don't you bring her in, we are just colleagues.'

'Oh yeah? She smooches you in public and it is splashed all across Page 3 and—'

'Hey, she just pecked me on the cheek on my birthday. It is the industry norm. Plus we have kissed on-screen many times, haven't we? What's the big deal?'

'Oh? So if the camera is on, anything becomes sacred? What if I do a movie and French-kiss Naresh and tell you that it is *just professional oral exploration for the advancement of the cause of modern cinema*?'

'Usha, please. The only exercise you seem to be getting these days is going mountain climbing over molehills—'

'Shut up! That's what *you* do! You are a hypocrite. Typical MCP. You can do anything, but your wife has to be a sindoor-sporting, pallu-draped-over-the-head, obedient lovebird caged inside the house, right?'

'I didn't say that. All I am saying is, please be careful about your choice of friends. We are celebs, dammit! I don't want to get my name dragged into any controversies. You know how the cops raid nightclubs and round up the druggies.'

'Enough of your paranoia! It's always about you. About how each and every act of mine has to revolve around your maintaining a goody-goody image in public. I don't care a damn about how you feel, Vishy! I have had enough of your snooping around through your media friends. Don't think I don't know that you'd sent John after me to the disc to spy on us—'

'I didn't send John. He was trying to find out if Shweta and Pavan are seeing each other. He was working on a scoop for next month's issue—'

'You expect me to buy your stupid story? Let's end this discussion right here. You do your thing and let me do mine. I am your wife, not your bonded labourer or slave, okay?'

'Okay, forget it. But be cautious—'

'There you go again like a CD on loop. Now stop behaving like Nana Patekar from *Agnisakshi*!'

I hated it when she went out anywhere without me. I mean, whenever she went out clubbing or partying when I wasn't around—not that I was against her visiting beauty salons or massage parlours. I had seen her hugging and kissing a few guys at some get-togethers at home, and she always kept saying that they were all good friends. Perhaps they were, but my obsession with Usha was becoming a tad pathological. I couldn't even object to her closeness with Naresh and gang because she could accuse me, too, of 'excessive social physical intimacy and public displays of affection with my female co-stars'.

This is what happens to all obsessive lovers, I guess. Love causes romance; romance causes marriage; marriage causes possessiveness; possessiveness causes suspicion; and suspicion grows like cancerous cells that kill love. Only large-heartedness and implicit trust in your mate can prevent this emotionally carcinogenic, self-destructive vicious cycle from taking charge of your mind and life. But then, I was neither large-hearted nor trusting.

෴

I was so angry with Usha that I badly wanted to fuck someone's trip, to get me swinging back into the groove. Jana and that so-called director Pavan—yes, they would do just fine, I thought. It was all long overdue anyway, especially considering how Jana had mocked my intelligence at the ghat, and also taking into account how Pavan had called me a dumb nightmare two weeks ago. The hisaab had to be barabaroed to make me feel good about myself. Unsettled accounts/scores cause insomnia. I had zeroed in on the prey. I was a predator ready to spin a trap, and sleep the sleep of a sated hunter.

I had sent my Mercedes driver to pick up Jana from Dadar railway station.

I was happy that Jana had taken the bait. He would reach me at my shoot in Film City in about an hour, depending on traffic.

I had made a nice plan to screw his life, and that of Pavan, too.

You will get to hear all about that as we chug along.

ॐ

We were shooting a song sequence that entailed lifting and twirling my heroine like a salsa dancer. But every time I held her by her waist and tried to lift her, my fingers encountered something greasy. I was wondering if the high-voltage lights were making her sweat more than normal.

'Cut!' shouted Pavan Mutreja, the debutant director, into a distant microphone. 'What the fuck, man! Why is she slipping like an eel from your arms? You need to do a bit of gymming, dude, can't even lift a petite girl or what?'

There he went again, the bloody sadist. I'd only accepted the movie to take this guy's case, but obviously he didn't know that. He'd acted funny with me in my second movie, when he was assisting Bawa, and I had decided then and there that I would befriend him and eventually sort him out by hurting him where it would sting the most: his professional aspirations.

ॐ

I had studied Pavan well—he liked reading highbrow books and watching obscure movies by Fellini and all, so over the past few months, I had given him many gifts, hobnobbed with him, gone to discos and pubs and filmy parties with him in tow, and had thus gained his confidence.

But familiarity and intimacy come with a dangerous side-effect: they make your acquaintances and friends take you for granted. These people begin to think that friendliness comes with a fundamental right to exude nastiness, and they justify this as a spontaneous sense of humour.

Every once in a while, at a party or private gathering, Pavan would put me down by saying 'Vishy is a brawny bozo who thinks that Fellini is a designer, like Armani', and his girlfriends would giggle. I'd pretend to be the generous type who loved laughing at weak, especially-directed-at-me jokes and one-liners. Usha had told me several times to stop moving around with Pavan, but then, she didn't know of my long-term plan.

Pavan had confessed to me on many occasions that it was his dream to be an ace director. He'd been working on some script for two years, and was waiting to rope in the right producer and financier. He had finally managed to find both. After that he had begged me to do the lead role in his debut flick, a comical thriller titled *Nau Numberi*.

I'd accepted Pavan's offer immediately, saying, 'Anything for you, buddy', and he had hugged me tightly and said, 'I knew I could always count on you, bro!' How wrong he had been about that!

To screw Jana's happiness along with Pavan's had been an afterthought. Thank heavens Pavan wasn't a mind-reader, or else he would have seen that my brain held more cunningness than can be found in the most depraved of moneylenders or pawn brokers, or the grinning munims of ancient Hindi movies who took great delight in tormenting impoverished widows, orphans and simpletons.

ॐ

But what the hell was the matter with this slippery girl's slippery waist? I felt as if I was trying to hold some giant slimy earthworm, bloody hell!

'Roopali! You've applied oil or something!' I accused the ravishing brunette.

'Nah, just a suntan lotion! Someone told me it would protect me from these lights that are so very dangerous for the skin, and also make my skin glow and look sexy on film—' she explained.

'Damn it, why have you applied that? Do you think you are vacationing in the Bahamas? Didn't you know about our salsa routine?' I said, pretending anger, though I was actually quite happy that the mercurial Pavan would blow a fuse or two because of the delay. We were on a tight schedule and budget, and every second counted. Every wasted minute meant a loss of a few thousand bucks and a gain of twenty systolic points on Pavan's stressed-out blood-pressure curve.

'Roopali! Go and get scrubbed immediately. Yogita, wash this woman's waist with Surf or Tide or something. Try acid if nothing else works...' ordered Pavan.

As Yogita vanished into the vanity van with Ms Suntan Lotion Waist, I saw Jana making his entry, with my driver guiding him towards me.

I remained where I was, pretending not to have noticed him. But my peripheral vision was taking him in. He looked around at the blinding lights, at the huge set simulating a waterfall and some snow-covered peaks, appearing totally out of place in his Fabindia kurta and trademark salt-and-pepper stubble. I hoped some idle spectators would come to take my autograph, so that Jana could clearly see how far ahead I had zoomed in life. Thankfully, a giggly bunch of girls approached me, extending their scribble pads and diaries, and I took my own sweet time before acknowledging Jana's presence.

'Hey, Jana, come on over, man!' I shouted cheerily at last, waving at him to join us.

He looked tired and lost.

I was happy to seem a towering success story compared to the dilapidated failure that he had become.

'Hi, you're looking good,' said Jana as we shook hands.

'You are the same,' I said, mocking his unkempt look. 'Some things never change.'

'Yeah,' he said tiredly.

'Okay, let's go to my vanity van,' I said, and turning to the bevy of autograph-hunters, 'Sorry, folks, gotta entertain my old pal now, catch you guys later.'

જ

'You'd like to have something, Jana?' I asked as I changed into designer Bermudas.

'Sure. Something to eat and drink would be most welcome,' said Jana.

'Long time, man! Feels like the good old times are back,' I said, thumping his shoulder patronizingly.

'Yeah...so how's Usha?'

'Oh, she's doing good for herself too! Call centre ops head and all that!'

'Good.'

'Damodar,' I said to my spot boy, 'get us some veg burgers and Diet Coke, and jaldi please.'

'*Theek hai, Sir, abhi laaya*,' said Damodar.

'Okay, Jana, listen, this is damn important. As you know, my first three movies were superhits. The fourth flopped. The fifth was a dud. Now this sixth *has* to do well! Everything hinges on this, man. This movie is shaping up well, but the bloody director, you know that guy Pavan, who was wearing that printed yellow shirt, he hasn't cracked the climax yet... well, at least not to my satisfaction. This is why I need you and your genius...'

I told Jana the storyline and the plot, with all its twists and turns, and he listened intently.

'Think you can crack the climax? You can make some easy money,' I urged.

Jana nodded and told me a simple Sufi story which I really liked.

'Fantastic story, dude! This is why I need you! Hey, this can be our climax!' I said.

'Yeah,' smiled Jana.

'Great show, Jana. Now you and Pavan can team up and iron out some loose ends in the plot. I will introduce him to you right away.'

ॐ

I had put Jana up at my manager's pad. It had a spare bedroom, which my manager used on weekends to deflower junior artistes who danced around the hero and heroine in Bollywood song sequences. A few weekends of celibacy wouldn't do my manager any harm—it might even improve his sex life, since cruel deprivation is the mother of consummate satisfaction. Anyway, who cared? I was the one who was paying the rent for the flat.

'You will have all the space to yourself to work on the script' was the spiel I had given Jana. I had also given him twenty grand as pocket change.

Over the days, Jana and Pavan formed a mutual admiration club of sorts—they both liked each other's creative instincts. Suited me just fine. Birds that flock together get screwed together.

I called up Jana at 8 a.m. one fine day, on the cell phone I had gifted him.

'Hey, hi, dude! Wassup?'

'Sleeping,' he said tiredly.

'Shouldn't you be working on the script?'

'Listen, I am not a vending machine. Ideas come when they come. My day begins late, and I am not answerable to you!'

'You are, Jana. I am your employer now.'

'Balls, I am just helping you.'

'I think it is the other way round. Even Sudama had to come to Krishna.'

'Did you get off the wrong side of the bed, Vishy?'

'Listen, dude, I just called up Pavan. He's coming over to your place. It's been two weeks now, and apart from the climax, I believe the other loose ends haven't been tied up yet—'

'It's all happening, stop breathing down my neck—'

'Hope so. I was thinking you could make about two lakh or something on this. So don't blow it. We both know how much you need the money.'

'I won't deny my cash flow problems, but you gotta be patient.'

'Okay, I'll give you guys time till tomorrow evening to come up with some good ideas. You and Pavan come over to my place after 9 p.m., okay?'

'Cool, I'll tell him that...'

'Bye, you better have something that excites my grey cells...'

'Let's see. Bye.'

ॐ

Pavan narrated the redone script to me for half an hour. He was quite animated and excited about it. I must confess, he and Jana had done a fantastic job of it, and if I hadn't had this devious plan to screw their trips in mind, I'd have loved to do the movie. But plans are plans, and like opportunities, they knock but once, so you got to focus and stick to the original strategy, lest the chance slip past.

'So isn't it fantastic?' asked Pavan gleefully. 'I tell you, Vishy, Jana is going to become a hotshot, much-sought-after scriptwriter after this one sets the screens ablaze...'

It was time to puncture them both.

'Well, Pavan, why have you guys introduced a new principal character *after* the interval?' I asked. 'It goes against the cardinal rule of scriptwriting...'

'That's called innovation,' said Jana.

'Yeah, there have been hundreds of movies with new characters showing up after the interval...' said Pavan.

'Sorry, even if I buy that argument, the way in which the hero arranges money on those seven occasions doesn't strike me as very plausible or logical...' I said.

'It's a movie, it has a logic all its own,' defended Jana.

'But where is the realism?' I countered.

'What realism? You seen *Zero No. 1*, dude? What logic was there? It was just fun, dude—' said Pavan.

'We are not making *Zero No. 1*, dumbo! We are making an action movie—' I replied.

'Action–comedy,' Jana corrected me.

'Vishy, you are splitting hairs unnecessarily, this is a super script,' said Pavan.

'Says who, Pavan? Even an ugly baby looks beautiful to its mother. It is the same with you guys...you both are suffering from the same emotional delusion...' I said.

'Listen, this movie's gonna rock...' argued Pavan.

'Says who?' I asked.

'I know scripts, I am the director, in case you have forgotten—' said Pavan.

'I think the script is the hero here...that is Vishy's problem—' said Jana.

'You think I will get overshadowed by your fuck-all script?' I pretended to yell.

'Vishy, let's do this, okay?' said Pavan.

'No, we don't, not as it has shaped up now!' I said.

'Man, we have already shot twenty per cent of the movie,' said Pavan.

'So what?' I said. 'I will return the signing amount to the producer—'

'Hey, this is my debut, man! You can't just walk out on me and screw my trip,' pleaded Pavan.

'Pavan, it is nothing personal, okay,' I lied. 'It is purely professional. Frankly, I thought Jana would make a good scriptwriter, but sorry Jana, you suck!'

'You can't ditch me like this, Vishy. You signed a contract—' said Pavan defiantly.

'Don't teach me legalities. You are forgetting that I was careful to include a conditional clause saying "if the script shapes up to Mr Vishnu Shankar's satisfaction" in the darned contract. What you say won't hold true in a court of law.'

'I am not talking law, I am talking friendship,' Pavan replied.

'Listen, dude, it is over. This movie is over. I am not doing it. Because, if it flops, it is my ass on the line, not yours, nobody even knows you guys—' I said.

'You are freaking me out, throwing starry tantrums just when I have announced my debut to the entire media—' shouted Pavan.

'Not my fault. You worked on it for two years, you said. But it is pathetic.'

'Then why did you agree to do it? You read the script!' said Pavan.

'Call it an error of judgement. I felt you'd weave something good later. Okay, guys, end of discussion, you wanna grab some drinks and dinner?'

'No, thanks, Vishy, I'll get going,' said Jana.

'Where are you going now?' I asked.

'Pavan, my sympathies are with you. This guy is a pathetic, sadistic, scheming bastard,' said Jana.

'Hey, mind your tongue!'

'Damn you, Vishy! Now I know what you had in mind all along. You never intended to do this movie. You just play-acted to screw us. I should have guessed it before, but I thought I'd give you the benefit of the doubt for once. But you are the same old sly fox! You are a slur upon humankind!'

'Just because you couldn't come up with a good idea, don't blame me!'

Jana didn't say anything and just walked away angrily.

Pavan pleaded with me for a while, and seeing that I wasn't relenting, walked away rather dejectedly.

Wow! You did it man! Jana got angry; Pavan got depressed. Serves the bastards right!

I fist-pumped the air and celebrated my cheap thrill by popping a bottle of Dom Perignon champagne.

Thankfully, Usha wasn't home, and would only come in late. She wouldn't have liked to see me hitting Jana below the creative belt.

༄

LEVEL 20

Fatal Attraction

Pleas for help might be booby traps—pun intended.

I took a long sabbatical to reassess my Bollywood career. Eight months, actually. Usha was happy that I had become a house-husband. We spent lots of time together, and even went to her dad's place in Allahabad for a month. As you no doubt know, my fourth movie had flopped dignifiedly a week after its release—so much for KAMP and Kabiji's confidence in the script; and the fifth had been a total dud. For an achiever, an alpha male wedded to his meteoric rise, any failure is an irritant. Falling from grace is sheer agony. You keep thinking of your failures for months on end. And you seldom think of the hits.

Plus, the media's relentless negative reportage during such times doesn't help either. The media never lets you forget your flops, even after decades. Initially, they worship a rising sun, like tribesmen marvelling at a magical phenomenon, and the moment your film flops, they deride you, like sadists yelling during a painful WWE match.

I was yet to sign my sixth movie after ditching Pavan—not that the offers had dried up—because I was doing detailed Six Sigma analyses on what had gone wrong with my two previous releases, and why the public hadn't liked them.

Money was not the issue, though. I had made enough and stashed away quite a bit already. But I was seriously concerned about my reputation as a bankable male lead. Bollywood works on sentiments, much like the stock market does, and if producers and directors perceive that your saleability has taken a beating, then they will look elsewhere or shortchange you on remuneration.

Since I was just sitting at home, I had become a bit of a couch potato. I was remote-surfing the networks and though I never liked spiritual bullshit, I still tuned into Omo channel—at least the spiritual mumbo-jumbo there seemed more genuine than filmy news or advertising or teleshopping.

Whew! What is this! It's him! I whistled slowly in amazement.

He was looking dapper in his red-robed, clean-shaven, tonsured look, and was delivering a discourse in English to a gathering of about 500 people gathered on the lawns of some obscure ashram.

Hell! Was that really Jana? Of course it was. The deep, confident voice was unmistakable.

His name was displayed as Swami Hasyavarahananda—he'd changed his name, too!

He was addressing a question-and-answer session. I listened in...

Q: What's the problem with the world?

A: This world is like a jar of dry fruits. There are too many nuts in it.

Q: What is our purpose in life?

A: You are not here to please anyone, you are here to please God.

Q: Why are so many miserable?

A: Because all want entertainment, almost no one wants enlightenment.

Q: How to tackle one's enemy?

A: Love thy enemy—and surprise him to death.

Q: What do you think of customs and traditions?

A: Customs are like cosmetics. They do not enhance beauty. They just hide blemishes. Likewise, traditions and customs are cosmetics in the world of pseudo-religion.

Q: How to reach God?

A: You can't reach God. God will have to reach you...

To be continued tomorrow at 7 a.m., said the screen.

Shucks, he made so much sense. I was missing him so much! It had been so soothing to just listen to him. My friend, my Jana, I wanted him back in my life!

ॐ

Usha would be checking in late again, and I was feeling darned lonely. I thought of calling up Harnoor but decided against it. I was in no mood for rubbing balm on her back and pleasuring that opportunistic slut.

My sabbatical had ended a month ago. I had been shooting for two movies at the same time for a while now, so my hands had been full. Though I did ensure that I got at least four offs a month from both units. I wanted at least three movies of mine released every year, and I had been slogging my butt off, juggling between sets and shooting schedules. The least I expected from Usha was that she would be at home when I returned, but usually she wasn't.

Oh, we also didn't see eye to eye on many other things.

I wanted her to be a homemaker, but she wanted to be a career girl.

I liked to have the AC on when we slept, but she always complained of a sinus problem, so we only used the ceiling fan. Yeah, we could have slept in different bedrooms, but she would sulk and become hysterical, saying I didn't love her anymore and that's why I couldn't even sacrifice a little comfort for her happiness. So, I had had to prove my love for her most nights by waking up drenched in sweat every morning.

I didn't want her giving a blow-by-blow account of our lifestyle and quarrels to my mom twice a week, but then, since Usha had lost her mother during her childhood, I guess she was looking for surrogate support.

I wanted to have kids soon, but she wanted us to go slow on family expansion plans.

The laundry list detailing the differences of opinion we had was endless, but so was my love for Usha. I guess love means understanding that it is a woman's world, after all. Love means voting for matriarchy. Love also means loving the way your woman uses you as an emotional toy and favourite punching bag. The Women's Liberation Movement would have made Usha their president or something if they had seen her walking all over me nearly every day.

I hated to discuss my work with anyone, but she loved to talk about office politics. 'You know how Sheena mothered

Chundu when he spoke *against* the Sexual Harassment Bill?' she'd say as she gave me a massage. Who cares? But I had to pretend I did. So I also had to keep nodding every time Usha asked, 'You do agree, don't you?' When a woman asks that, don't mistake it for a question, because it is actually a command that means: 'You'd better agree.'

I loved Usha so much, but I didn't want to spend too much time with her. I knew that sooner or later, we would get into an argument when my patience reached the end of its tether. I didn't want that to happen. So I immersed myself in work. Now you know why I had been shooting for two movies at the same time.

Well, get married to the woman you love at your own risk. They say love is blind. No, it is not. You can clearly see what is happening; only you can't do anything about it. Love is dumb—it makes you tongue-tied, helpless, speechless and paralysed.

Love is slow death—you feel as good as dead if you *don't* get the girl you want; and your individuality and personality are killed systematically if you *do* get the girl you want. Either way, you are screwed—literally and existentially.

Sometimes I wonder if Jana was right when he had expounded upon the subject of love one night at the ghat. 'You know, Vishy, there are only five things a man ought to actually love—his intelligence, wisdom, soul and God,' he'd said.

'And what's the fifth?' I'd asked.

'The fifth is complete freedom from the first four loves. Wanting neither himself, nor God, nor enlightenment, nor nirvana nor anything—that is Buddhahood,' he'd said.

'But I want Usha,' I'd said.

'Remember, what begins as nectar will end up becoming poison,' he'd said.

'Jana, you are such a cynic,' I'd said.

'Better than being a puppet,' he'd replied.

Well, I was still a puppet of Usha's moods and desires and likes and dislikes, but she had grown indifferent. I couldn't imagine life without her now. Thankfully, my cell rang to prevent me from torturing myself further with thoughts on my failing marriage, shattered desires and contradictory feelings of love.

Aha, Nimika.

'Hi! Wassup!' I said.

'Vishy, I am feeling so down and out—'

'Join the gang, buddy, so am I—'

'Come over, na, let's talk and chill out for a while.'

'Okay, in half an hour, bye.'

When Nimika opened her door, she was wearing peach lingerie and a desolate expression. Well, I had seen much more of her in public, when we'd done our semi-naked swimming scene in our first movie, but she was looking quite sexy today. I wondered why her career hadn't taken off—she had more oomph, beauty and acting skills than the top five Bollywood heroines, but then, it is all destiny, kismet.

Nimika gave me a peck on the cheek and a bear hug. I returned the favour and we snuggled up on her couch.

'Drink?' she asked.

'Sure,' I said. 'What do you have?'

'Cognac okay with you?'

'Super.'

We sat together like good friends, drinking and chatting about old times, and laughing at our insecurities and my recent flops.

After an hour or so, I felt so zonked that I forgot who I was.

What the hell was happening?

When I woke up after a while, I was stunned to see that I was lying next to Nimika on her bed! Shit, I was stark naked, too!

I checked my Rolex chronograph placed on the bedside table. 3.55 a.m.

What the hell had happened? When did I take off all my clothes? Shit, hope she hadn't seen me like this! Hope I didn't do anything stupid! Anyway, she was snoring, and I consoled myself by thinking that I had doffed all my clothes after she'd fallen asleep...

I got into my jeans and T-shirt hurriedly, and exited her apartment.

When I got off the lift downstairs, two journos clicked snaps of me. The flash was blinding.

Why were the paparazzi there? Didn't they ever sleep? Were they nocturnal vampires mutated as humans?

'What the hell are you doing, you idiots?' I asked angrily.

'Vishy, what were you doing in Nimika's flat so late in the night?' asked Journo 1.

'Discussing a script, none of your bloody business...' I said gruffly.

'Yeah, yeah, just good friends,' said Journo 2, laughing.

'Buzz off, both of you!' I shouted.

I rushed to the parking lot and whizzed past them even as they clicked more snaps of me.

⌒

Usha had dozed off by the time I reached home. I, however, couldn't sleep. I switched on the TV and watched some idiotic Hollywood movie. Then I remembered that Jana's discourse would begin at 7 a.m. It was 4.16 a.m. now. Just a few more hours to kill. I was dying to hear him again. Listening to him would soothe my nerves—like always.

Should I tell Usha about what had happened, when she woke up? What would I say? That I was stark naked with Nimika in her bed? And that I don't know how it had all happened? *What a locha!* Hope the paparazzi would be afraid of my filing a defamation suit, and would decide against publishing anything that would seriously damage my reputation. I was petrified...

Eventually, Jana reappeared on screen. How peaceful and serene he looked. I would have loved to trade places with him...

He was again addressing a Q&A session that morning.

Q: What is the greatest disease afflicting humankind?

A: Comparisons.

Q: I get overwhelmed by emotions. What to do?

A: Nothing. There is nothing you can do about it. Every emotion you feel is infinite. Can you say I am 88.6 per cent angry or 92.7 per cent in love or 48.3 per cent happy? All emotions are totalitarians. They believe in total dominion. They will overpower you till you get enlightened.

Q: Why do people tell lies?

A: Because the truth is dangerous. It is actually suicidal. The truth will destroy the false you, but all have made great investments in being the false themselves. They have created a fake persona and wish to preserve this at all costs. Unless someone is suicidal, he or she can't live the truth all the time, but it is far better to die for the truth rather than live lies...

To be continued tomorrow at 7 a.m.

That's exactly what I was living: lies.

Jana might as well have been talking about me. Was he? Did he even think of me? I had cheated on Usha when I slept with Harnoor. I had cheated Jana and Pavan when I sent them on a creative, fruitless, script-doctoring pursuit. I had been a diplomatic, scheming, manipulative, cunning monster...

What had I become? Was I even human?

I was beginning to feel so inadequate that I could have hanged myself right then.

No, get a grip on yourself. This is how 99 per cent of the world is. There is security in numbers. And in a healthy bank balance. And in fame. Don't get influenced by Jana again! Your mission is to be India's No. 1 film star. To take the shortcut to success, you have to sacrifice principles and loyalty and truth, and all that shit. Don't lose focus now. Be what you are. Balls to Jana and his philosophy!

∿

I was waiting for Usha to wake up. I had decided to tell her that I was with Nimika till late in the night. The media might report it anytime, and just knowing that I had mentioned it casually would make me seem more credible than whatever reportage the media carried.

Usha got up rather late. I was digging into my favourite breakfast of luchi and aloo dum.

'Hi, honey! Morning!' she said, wrapping her arms around me from behind.

'Hi, Q2! You were asleep when I returned. Didn't wish to disturb your beauty sleep—'

'Where were you, honeypie?'

'Oh, I was with Nimika. Discussing a script—'

'Oh, cool, so how is she? Not giving you the glad eye, I hope—'

'C'mon, you know we are just good friends. But she is a tad unhappy that she's not made it the way I have... She sent you her regards—'

'She's a nice sort, Vishy, but I think she should step out of her glamorous image to be taken as a serious actress. I guess she should do one or two parallel cinema stuff. You know, low-budget things with a meatier screen presence. She's too good an actress to do skin shows and bikini scenes—'

'Yeah, I told her just that. Hey, I saw Jana on TV—'

'I know, he's a hotshot guru now. Omo channel, right?'

'You know about it? Why didn't you tell me then?'

'I thought you didn't want to discuss Jana...you get irked whenever I mention him, so I thought it was better not to—'

'Okay, okay, forget it. Let's talk about us, Q2.'

'So what are your plans for the day?'

'Nothing special. Why?'

'It's my day off, honey! Let's chill somewhere!'

We decided to drive down to Khandala to spend the day at the farmhouse of a director friend of mine.

Well, I had an ulterior motive in meeting Shantanu Rai. He had sounded me about his next movie, and was eager to cast me. I had to take a slight pay cut, and I had told him that I would think about it and let him know later. That discussion had happened last week. He had told me that he was planning to shoot in exotic locales in South America, and right now I wished to get out of Mumbai real fast. We could even discuss the script while we chilled out at his farmhouse.

I called up Shantanu and he was happy to invite me over.

His script was no great shakes: the same clichéd action, comedy, dialogues, song-and-dance routines, but I still decided to do it because suddenly, I felt like going far, far, far away from Mumbai.

He said that the unit would be flying abroad in about two weeks' time.

That suited me just fine.

LEVEL 21

Cast Away

The worst pain is feeling like an orphan while your parents are still alive.

A month later, my worst fears came true. I found myself in bigger trouble than I'd anticipated. I was out on the shoot I'd talked about earlier, and had to return urgently from Mexico as Usha faked a medical emergency on the long distance call: 'I am going crazy, and am definitely headed for depression, so come back fast,' she said. 'Drop everything right now and to hell with the shoot!'

She summoned me back because for the past one week I was being hounded by the press in India—you know why.

Usha saw the news items first in the bloody tabloids and film magazines, which are forever prying into and ripping apart the lives of celebs and their wives. That's an occupational hazard for film stars like me—comes with the territory, I guess. We need the media for publicity, for the precious sound bytes to push our movies into people's minds. The media needs us to push their dailies and mags and filmy programmes into people's minds. And the people need both the media and us to push their fucked-up lives *out* of their fucked-up minds. What a perverted, symbiotic, vicious cycle! Reminds me of what Arpita had said to Neelima many moons ago—life is one long sales trip, and we are all whores.

Usha had scanned some reports and sent me a few email attachments. So very kind of her to rub it in.

Something fishy in Vishy's life/Another 'wife' in Vishy's life?/Kahani mein twist—Nimika pregnant?

I read much the same on the Internet. And more.

The unit was silent about it. My new heroine suddenly became a bit cold with me. Shantanu was accommodating, though.

'Vishy, just go, sort this out, and return in a week,' he said.

'Thanks, dude,' I said, 'but what if I am not able to return—you know how stubborn Usha can get.'

'Cool, I can handle that,' said Shantanu. 'I will just shoot the scenes where you aren't required. Most of your song sequences are canned already. Don't worry about this movie—go handle your life and wife, man!'

I called up Usha to calm her down and said that I was leaving right away.

Usha said that she was sitting glued to the television, and every time she surfed channels, I was there for all the wrong reasons.

Damn! The media is always trying to boost its TRPs and forever titillating the collective cerebrum with some juicy scandals. And I had been such an idiot. I had provided them with the ideal gossip fodder, stuff that would generate a billion conversational orgasms at a million kitty parties across India.

What do I do now?

Mom called and I denied it.

Some press people called me up from India and I denied it.

I denied it to myself, too.

I was in denial—totally, utterly, completely.

No, it had never happened the way it was being reported. I had just gone to help Nimika and lend her a patient ear like a good friend. Had I lent her more of my anatomy than my ear? Should I file a defamation suit against her? Hell, no. What if she filed a rape case instead? I remembered zilch about what had happened that night. Should I call her up? No way, I was not going to talk to that bitch ever again. Just thinking about her was making me feel nauseated...

But how long could I continue the lie?

At least Usha had to be told the truth. There was no other way.

The long-haul journey from Mexico to Mumbai, with two not-so-brief stopovers at New York and Frankfurt and two plane changes, was the worst trip of my life. I was gripped by an unbearable fright.

Would Usha leave me? What the hell would I do without her? Would she forgive me my lapse? No, she was much too headstrong for that. Surely she would walk away from me. How would I bear it? God! What could I do to repair the hellish situation I had got myself into?

ॐ

'You bastard! Tell me the truth!' she screamed.

'Usha, please, at least let me settle down first,' I said, sinking into the living room sofa.

'Balls, don't stall for time, your energy levels never suffer jet lag and all!'

'I am not talking jet lag, Q2. Please, I am sorry—'

'Did you or did you not sleep with Nimika?'

'It is not like what you think, honey! And you don't look a wee bit depressed to me, you look angry—'

'Spare me your psychoanalysis. I lied, okay? To have you fly down fast. Did you sleep with her or not? Just say yes or no!'

'Listen, it is more complicated than that...she had called me over saying she was feeling rather low one night... remember, I told you about it? We went to Shantanu's farmhouse the next day? And she said she wanted my help, and I—'

'Damn you, Vishy! I want no lengthy explanations! Did you make out with her, and did you make her pregnant or not? Say no and I will believe you!'

'I can't say no!'

'Then say yes!'

'I can't say yes, either!'

'What the bloody hell?'

'Q2, I don't remember what exactly happened that night...we had a few drinks and—'

'The press is saying that she's claiming she's carrying your love child! She's saying she's been having an affair with you for two years now!'

'That's a bloody lie! Some people are conspiring against me! I have never had any affair with her. Just one bloody night—'

'So it was a one-night stand?'

'It is not like that...I guess I was drugged by her that night...she is doing this for cheap publicity, the bloody bitch!'

'She is saying they can do a paternity test later if they don't believe her, and you are still denying it?'

'I am not denying it, Usha. Okay, I *think* I slept with her that night... It could have happened, I am not too sure—'

'That does it, Vishy. It is over.'

'What do you mean, it is over?'

'You heard me. *Us* is over!'

ॐ

After Usha walked out on me, I gave a fully-paid holiday to all my assistants, drivers, servants and live-in maids because I wanted to be left all alone. Grief, guilt and regrets are best suffered in solitude.

Only Mamta seemed to be worried about leaving me alone during such trying times; all the others seemed to be happy that they could steal a bit of quality time with their families in distant suburbs, towns and villages. Mamta made me promise her that I would eat well, drink less and generally take good care of myself. She was nearly fifty and functioned liked a caring granny.

'Vishu baba,' she said to me when she left rather reluctantly for her village in UP, *'sab theek ho jayega.'*

I lived like a zombie, and told my directors and producers that I was not going to do a single scene or dubbing for at least a few months. They said that it would be good if I took a month or two off before swinging back into action.

A week later, Dad called me up, saying he and Mom were coming over.

I offered to pick them up from the airport, but he said he would hire a taxi.

When Dad and Mom checked in, I was a bit sozzled.

'So,' said Dad, without much preamble, 'is it true?'

'Yes, Papa, I am sorry,' I said sheepishly.

That's when Dad slapped me.

'You incorrigible idiot!' he yelled. 'Just because you are a big film star, you think you can do anything you feel like?'

I remained silent, with my eyes downcast. I hadn't felt so low even when he had belted me black and blue for punching a guy and breaking his nose when I was in class six—that, after I had untied that guy's sister's ribbon and pinched her bottom. The principal had called Dad that day and I had come close to being expelled, I learnt later, but Dad had monetarily compensated the school and the two victims generously. Dad had also sought forgiveness from the students' folks, so I had just been transferred to a different section—which, incidentally, had better girls to ogle.

Dad was livid now. He wasn't going to bail me out of this one because adultery is a slightly more serious affair (pun intended) than pre-teen violence and bottom-pinching episodes.

'Please, what's done is done,' Mom said, defending my adultery. 'It's all youthful blood.'

In my case, there is more testosterone than RBCs in the bloodstream, I thought. If I wasn't feeling like a piece of shit, I'd have at least smiled at my wry observation.

'You keep quiet, Kala! Youth! What youth? This fool gets his looks only because I am handsome and you are beautiful. And he has abused his freedom. Haven't we experienced youth?' thundered Dad. 'Have we ever done anything immoral? He has made that girl pregnant! Mr Tripathi called me up and...and...you know what he said? "Mr Majumdar, your son has ruined a life, maybe more, but I have forgiven him. Though I am sure God will not! I am really sorry that you have such a pathetic, pathological, paapi son like Vishy. Please accept my condolences and sympathies!" Is this why you gave birth to him, Kala? So people can offer us condolences and sympathies for raising a devil?'

Mom just kept looking at me, perhaps wondering if supporting me now would worsen matters.

'Papa, I am sorry—' I said.

'A mere sorry won't undo the harm you have done us all. Enough, Kala. I am leaving. Come,' said Dad, and made for the door.

'Please, let's talk to him, he needs us in this hour of crisis—' she said to Dad, but he wasn't listening to the voice of maternal reason.

'I will wait for you downstairs for exactly five minutes,' said Dad, looking at his Casio digital watch. 'If you don't come by then, you are welcome to stay here with him. If I can disown this rascal, Kala, then I can do the same to you, too. You decide who you want to be with!'

'Please, let us at least...' pleaded Mom, but he had left.

'Mamma, I am sorry,' I said.

She took me in her warm embrace and cried. I photocopied her wails and we stood there entwined for about a minute: she, wondering silently if my life would sort itself out; I, knowing that it wouldn't.

'Vishy, shona, don't worry, everything will be okay,' she said, kissing my cheek, more to console herself than me, and wiping my tears with the pallu of her sari.

'Mamma, now go, Papa is very angry. Don't worry, I will handle myself,' I said.

'*Bhaalo theko.* And promise me you won't do anything drastic,' she sobbed.

'Mamma, please, don't worry, I will live with the pain. I deserve it,' I assured her, allaying her fears that I'd end my life or something.

She released me with great difficulty and willpower (perhaps after experiencing a rare tussle between unconditional love for errant son vs. phenomenal respect for principled hubby; the latter won the internal wrestling match, of course).

As she walked out of the door, she didn't look back and I knew why. Mothers don't like to see their sons looking beaten, fallen and defeated. I chose not to escort her downstairs as she pressed the elevator button. She wiped her face with her sari as she got into the elevator and I knew that that was the last I would see of her in a long, long while.

I fixed myself my umpteenth drink (a Campari on the rocks, if I remember right, which I'd picked up on a shoot in Italy) and slumped over my desk. Writing was so cathartic. I wrote Usha a long email, asking her to '...kick me, beat me, slap me, holler at me—but please don't ignore me like this...your silence is so deafening and killing, Q2...'

Someone rang the doorbell when I had nearly nodded off. I looked up at the clock. It was an hour after Dad and Mom had left. Who could it be? Had Usha come back? 'No way, stop deluding yourself,' I mumbled as I staggered to the door.

It was the gorkha.

'*Haan? Kya chahiye*?' I asked irritatedly.

'*Saab, aapke daddy ne yeh cover diya hain.*' He handed over an envelope.

'*Theek hai, shukriya,*' I said, readying to shut the door as he salaamed me.

The envelope carried a key and a handwritten letter.

Mr Vishnu Shankar,
I am hereby returning your car that was given to me, and your gifts given to my wife.

The boxes and bundle in the glove box contain all the gold bangles and diamond necklaces and precious rings you purchased for my wife.

I am not in the habit of retaining things given by scoundrels. I will not let my house be polluted by filth given by an immoral person like you.

Also, there is a cheque for ₹7,20,000 only—deposit it and withdraw the money, or I will have someone send the cash to you in a week's time—I calculated that you had also sent this amount to my wife and me over the past two years.

Needless to say, you will not contact either of us in this lifetime, and hopefully, in no future lifetime either. Consider us dead and we will return the favour to you.

Yes, there are a few other saris and clothes and some gifts, etc. Some have been disposed of and all others will be disposed of this week. I am making a rough calculation of all that, too. I think you must have spent something like ₹300,000 on them. That is a separate amount.

Since you must have spent cash to buy them, you can find a few 500-rupee and 100-rupee bundles in the briefcase kept below the backseat on the left.

If this amount is insufficient, let me know. I will reimburse the deficit amount, too. Take it, throw money around and go get a few more girls pregnant. I am sure there is no dearth of women with loose morals in your circles. Good. Filthy birds of the same feather should filthily flock together.

I didn't want to give all this in front of my wife since she is so stupidly sentimental.

I don't want to keep any of your childhood photographs and other stupid memories of your youth, either—you will receive all of your things by courier in a day or two.

I am ashamed that you carry our DNA and genes—but there is no way I can take that back.

This is my last communication to you.

Consider yourself disowned; and us, definitely dead.

Late Mr Majumdar

I howled for a long while. I had lost everything. Usha, Mom, Dad...everything gone! Everything that ever mattered was gone!

I went down to the parking lot after about half an hour. There. The Toyota Corolla I had gifted Dad on his last birthday stood there: a cruel reminder of the fact that I had finally been officially disowned by the Majumdars.

I sat holding the steering wheel for a while. The interior still smelt of Dad. The spiritual scent of vibhuthi, the unmistakable fragrance of burnt incense sticks and the small marble statue of Krishna reminded me of Karol Bagh. I suddenly wanted to be that gawky, silly, dumb teenager being scolded by Dad. I suddenly wanted to regain my boyhood, dump Bollywood and go back home. At least I had had them with me then. I tried holding back my tears as I clicked open the glove box. I couldn't. (I mean I couldn't hold back the tears, dumbo—even an infant can open a glove box.) Inside were three jewellery boxes and a small cloth bundle.

I felt like taking the Toyota for a spin and plunging it into some lake/skydiving with it on some Lonavala slope/ramming it into a high-velocity train. (What do you recommend? Something even better? Should we co-author a book titled *108 Cool Ways to End Your Life*?)

Was life worth living any longer? What would I do with money and fame? The only people I really loved—Usha and Mom and Dad—had left me, perhaps forever.

No, hang on, be bold, be strong, you promised your mom that you'd live on and take the pain, didn't you? Haven't you said on many occasions that people who don't handle crises with fortitude are feather-brained cowards? Take it, take the pain—it is repentance! You took the good times,

*now take the bad. Exactly what Billy Joel sang in 'Just The
Way You Are'. Be a man. What did Jana's brilliant poem
say? Suicide is never right/Don't escape your plight/Stay and
fight/All day, all night...*

I collected the stuff and staggered back to my pad.

I flopped on the bed and burst like a dam whose sluice
gates are thrown open suddenly.

ॐ

Usha hadn't called or texted, and I couldn't bear the
separation. She had switched off her cell phones, too.
Perhaps she was shacking up with a friend I didn't know
about, so that I couldn't trace her. Or perhaps she had gone
to her father's place in Allahabad. Or maybe she had gone
off to Pune.

I wrote her email after email but she didn't reply for
a long while... Then, after a fortnight or so, she replied,
saying she would come to meet me the next day. Ah,
there was a glimmer of hope! We could talk things out!
I suddenly felt alive! Should I fix an appointment with a
marriage counsellor? No, Usha would hate that. Should I
reserve a table at Olive? No, she wouldn't agree to dine out.
Okay, I would just order her fave takeaway: paneer frankies
and cheeseburgers from The Unrestaurant just round the
corner.

When she dropped by in the evening, I felt sorry for
her. And for myself. She looked distraught and confused.
Her eyes had sunk a bit into their sockets. Gone was her
glow, her air of happiness. What the hell had I done to the
only woman I so deeply loved?

'Hi, Q2,' I said as I let her in.

'Hi.'

'So how've you been?'

'Not too good, but that's okay.'

'Listen, we can still—'

'Shut up! You do the listening!'

'Okay.'

'Jana convinced me to—'

'Damn Jana! He's a bastard!'

'Damn you, Vishy! He's a gem. It is only because of him that I am even talking to you. Do you know what all he has done for you?'

'What has he done except brainwash you into disliking me?'

She didn't say anything. Instead, she showed me an email printout:

Dear Usha,

Read this with an open mind. Please don't bring your emotions into it.

Despite all his faults, Vishy is a decent guy. He might be egoistic, arrogant, selfish and success might have gone to his head and all—I am not denying any of this—but deep down he has a pure and generous heart. (Trust me, I am good at reading people. So are you, Usha, the purest amongst us.)

Come on, anyone can make a mistake in a moment of weakness, and we should understand that.

I know it will be difficult for you to forget the Nimika episode, but I am imploring you to forgive him and move on for your own good.

Accidents can happen to anyone; and one-off adulterous episodes also happen just like that.

You don't junk your Mercedes because someone you don't like sat in it for a while...

I know that is a stupid analogy, but it just crossed my mind that we tend to junk people on the slightest pretext.

Think of all the good times you had together... think of your budding romance at Goratown Park... think of how Vishy stood up for you at Cosmos...

Do not let a single pimple make you hate your entire face... Do not let a single rotten incident sour your entire life...

Vishy loves you and no one else. I know this.

Yes, he might have been lusting after other women, but when it comes to love, I know that that is an emotion he feels only for you—apart from loving himself and his parents, of course.

And I know that you also love him.

You have a right to be angry with him but you don't have the right to ruin both your lives thus.

You guys are made for each other—and I will be extremely happy and indebted to you if you can at least talk it out with him. Being silent and brushing issues under the carpet will not help.

Scream at him, beat him up, why, even throw a rolling pin at him, he deserves it, but talk to him, please.

He needs you. You need him. And I need you both to be happy.

Drop the past, Usha. Create a new future together.

Your best friend (who's also living your pain, and trust me, it hurts me no end to see you wonderful people drifting apart thus...and Vishy's best friend too, though he wouldn't want to believe it... Take care, buddy)

Jana

PS: Please don't discuss this mail with him. He will think I am trying to earn brownie points or he might fly off the handle even on hearing my name. God bless both of you.

'So? He wrote a mail. What does that prove?' I said, angry that she was in touch with Jana.

'That's not all. He spoke to my dad and sorted out many things,' said Usha.

'So? All that was only to make him look good in your eyes! All that was only to make you fall for him!'

'How dare you! You are pathetic, Vishy! How can you insinuate something like this about Jana? Do you think he's trying to do all this to enhance his stock with me? What an idea!'

'Okay, forget Jana, what about us now?'

'Well, I thought you'd be a changed person but I can see that you aren't.'

'Changed what? Okay, I made a mistake. So have many men. And many women. So what? Let's move on, and don't ask me: what if you had done the same? The answer is, I don't know. Perhaps my love for you would have made me forgive you—'

'Reminds me a bit of *Arth*.'

'Yeah, good movie. Look, Usha, I love you. Now, do you love me?'

'I still love you, Vishy. And that's the reason we can't stay together anymore.'

'Why? It is love only if it can endure anything!'

'No, Vishy. Every time you'll go on shoots, every time you'll cavort with your heroines, I will feel suspicious, and no amount of convincing from your side will help—'

'But nothing like that will ever happen again, I promise!'

'I agree, it might not happen at all. But I can't live with the constant fear that it might. Unless—'

'Unless what?'

'Unless you promise to quit movies and... Okay, let's start a call centre or something...so we can always be together... then there is a chance for us to also work together...and put all this Bollywood bullshit past us...but as long as you are in the movies, forget it—'

'Usha, please, do you know how much I have endured in life? How much I have been ridiculed by my father and others throughout my teenage years? How can I give up all this? Running a call centre is balls! There I will be a slave of some firang clients. We know that. Here, I am the king! C'mon, honey!'

'Vishy, enough. Money and fame are more important than me? Then say so!'

'Hey, I didn't mean it that way. What is mine is yours also. We are in this together. It is our money and our fame! Is this Jana's idea?'

'No, mine. Okay, not a call centre, we can do something else, some other business, but unless you quit movies, we can't be together.'

'Please, Usha, I need you with me, I have been going crazy without you.'

'So have I...but this is final...yes or no?'

'Life can't be decided by a single yes or no! Things are grey, okay? Not black and white! You are asking me to give up everything I have ever dreamed of: money, fame, success, adulation, every damn thing!'

'Okay, I got my answer.'

'No you didn't! We need this, Usha. You know how we had to scrounge to buy the simple things. Remember how we used to get elated by the few crumbs Duniya used to throw at us? Hell, we are now the eighth or ninth power couple in Bollywood! Give me a chance, please...that was a moment of weakness with Nimika...I was drunk that night, totally sloshed, maybe even drugged...I don't know...I still can't recall what exactly happened—'

'Enough of your bunkum story! Alcoholic misdemeanours don't justify adultery! I trusted you, you sex maniac! Even when you were doing all those bloody intimate scenes, I was so generous...and...and you go and break my trust in you, jeopardize our relationship, as if I am a bloody sexual soup, an appetizer or something that you taste a bit...whereas the main course is elsewhere!'

'It happened only once, Usha, don't make it seem as I was sleeping with her for months at a stretch—'

'Even murder happens just once. You can't tell a person, "Hey, after all, I killed you only once, I promise not to repeat the act." If the paparazzi hadn't caught you guys, if the MMS hadn't been leaked, which you neatly covered up by saying you were rehearsing for a scene...then even months might have gone by... Hell, what a pathetic cover-up, the heights of depravity—' (Sorry, it skipped my mind, Nimika had recorded my intimacy with her on her cell, and leaked out the MMS...anyway, forget it, just thinking about it makes my blood boil... I had called up the bitch from Mexico, and she'd said that now I must divorce Usha and marry her, after which we'd had a long telephonic showdown...I feel nauseated even thinking that Nimika could stoop so low...)

'Where was the choice? I had to cover up! But did I lie to you? Didn't I confess to you as soon as I landed in India?'

'So? You think you did me a great favour? What if I offer myself to some Tom, Dick—pun intended—or Harry, and confess later? That would set things right?'

'No, it wouldn't. Listen, we are going in circles—'

'And you were so stupid to cover up... That bloody bitch told the media that she's carrying your love child and you should have been man enough to accept it immediately.'

'Arre, how was I to know that? How could I have known she'd make it brazenly public! Her career didn't take off. Mine did, and she just used me for some cheap publicity... and perhaps to ride a sympathy wave—'

'Do you know that she plans to have the baby?'

'I know, what am I supposed to do about that? I can't force her to abort at gunpoint...I can't give a supari for her and get her bumped off or something... I have tried talking her out of it, but she is adamant...I have even offered money, but she doesn't want it—'

'What does the bloody bitch want then?'

'Me.'

'I knew it! So you now want to divorce me and marry her, right? How very convenient!'

'Q2, please. I can't. I am never going to marry anyone if you leave me. Please, don't even think like that. Let's sort out this mess we have got ourselves into—'

'*We?*'

'I mean me... Okay, I got us into this shit, okay, I am to blame obviously, but please, even Dad has abandoned me, Mom has gone with him...you are the only one I can call family...and if you also leave me, then what do I have left?'

'Your ego! Your damned ego will keep you company!'

'It is not ego. I am just being practical. Acting comes easily to me. Plus, the money is good. That's the reason I can't quit.'

'All liars make good actors.'

'Usha, enough! I can't quit movies.'

'But you can quit me—'

'I need both! That's like bread, you are butter—'

'And if God says you can have only one at a time?'

'What will we do, Usha? I can't even think of doing anything else...please try to understand...I am begging you...please don't ask hypothetical, impossible questions... we need both eyes to see properly...a bird needs both wings...I need to be an actor *and* stay married to you, to be happy.'

'Are you going to quit films or not?'

'Usha, please, I will quit films eventually—'

'*No! Now! Today! Right this minute!*'

'You are asking for the impossible.'

'Okay, I got my answer. Goodbye and good luck. Have a great, filmy life!'

'Please...plleaasse stay...I need you—' (Was I beginning to sound like George Michael in *Careless Whispers*?)

'Stop acting! Reserve it for the cameras! You will get my notice soon.'

'You can't send me a divorce notice now.'

'Why?'

'It hurts me to even consider that...I will die, Usha!'

'I am already dead. You have killed me, Vishy. I don't think I can ever feel alive again...but don't worry, I won't ask for any severance amount or alimony...all the money is yours—'

'Q2, we will start a new life, full of fun and love and laughter... C'mon, be a sport...please forgive me this once—'

'Dead women don't talk. Bye.'

The Three Musketeers

Old friends are far more soothing than old wine.

hree days after my failed attempt to woo back Usha, I began writing my autobiography. What could I do? When I put pen to paper, when I began speaking to you, dear reader, I somehow felt cleansed. It was a bit like a couch session with a shrink. I wrote like a man possessed by Shakespeare's ghost...

The doorbell rang for a long while. I was still jotting down my thoughts...

Must be the maid or the cook or the Audi driver who is always splurging money on matka, and forever rushing to me for some advance to bail him out... I think I ought to fire him... Or perhaps it is the watchman inviting me to some silly housing society meeting on Sunday... Gosh, there's not a moment of peace in this city...I think I ought to migrate to some desolate desert to be left alone... Could it be Usha having had a change of mind and heart? Ah, that would be heaven... Stop it, Vishy, she's not going to come back to you, unless something miraculous happens...

As I looked into the video door phone, I couldn't believe my eyes. I looked again to see if my muzzy, alcohol-soaked brain was spinning some kind of illusory, triple apparition.

Arpita and Neelima and Bijlee?

No, it couldn't be! But it indeed was!

I opened the door hungrily—starved as I had been of warm, friendly, affectionate company for quite some days now. Nothing like old pals to tide over a bad phase—works better than Campari, as I would discover later.

'Hey, wow! The three musketeers! What a pleasant surprise! Come on in...' I shrieked.

Neelima and Arpita gave me a huge hug. Bijlee sized me up quietly.

'So how come all of you landed up at the same time?' I wondered aloud.

'Well, cut the crap and pleasantries, Vishy,' said Neelima. 'Why are you screwing up your wonderful life?'

'Yeah, the tabloids and mags are full of how you've become a compulsive alcoholic who's on the road to self-destruction...' added Arpita.

'Hey, c'mon guys, you know how it is. The media just spins yarn to increase sales,' I defended my pathetic situation.

'Yeah, yeah, the media is responsible for everything from flintstones and sparks to smoke without fire,' said Bijlee in his trademark sarcastic manner.

'Shut up, Bijlee!' said Neelima. 'Look, Vishy, initially we also thought it was just media hype, but Arpi mailed Usha, so we realized how serious your troubles were, and then we coordinated our trips to spend some quality time with you—'

'Hey, thanks, I appreciate that, Neelu; by the way, where are your bags? You came without any overnighters?' I asked.

'We checked in at the Ginger, didn't know if you'd be comfy with us here,' said Arpi.

'Oh, c'mon, I'm lonely as hell, it'd be great to have you folks around,' I said.

'Okay, we'll move in,' said Neelima. 'Now tell us what happened.'

So I told them everything that had happened between Nimika and me that fateful night.

They listened calmly and attentively. I felt better.

'Okay, is there any way to calm down Usha?' asked Bijlee.

'Not a chance in hell, I got a mail from her yesterday evening, and she is definitely filing for divorce, unless of course—' Arpita broke off mid-sentence and looked at me searchingly.

'Yeah I know, unless I stop doing movies, she told me,' I said.

'Hmm, and you refused?' said Neelima.

'Obviously, Neelu, he's come a long way, we all know that, can't chuck it all for just damn-all sentiments like love and marriage,' said Bijlee.

'Shut up, you woman-hater!' said Arpita.

'Well, Usha is being a bit unreasonable here—it is not as if you were having a lifelong affair, just a one-night mistake thing,' said Neelima to me.

'Neelu, don't talk nonsense. Usha is pretty conservative and all, also, the filmy mags have made her a bit of a laughing stock, so her stance is justified,' observed Arpita.

'Hey, those are just Pavan's contacts and all...they are misusing their media contacts to sabotage whatever little chance I have with her—' I said.

'Who is Pavan now? One of Usha's close friends?' asked Arpita.

'Hell, no, just a director whose movie I refused to do since he couldn't get the climax right, so he's trying to get even indirectly—'

'Okay, I need a beer. Vishy, you got any?' asked Arpita.

'Yeah, sure, I will get it for you,' I said, getting up.

'No, please, just tell me where it is,' said Arpita.

'Cool, it's in the Samsung fridge, the LG has exotic stuff...' I said.

'Arpi, get us a Coke, while you are at it,' said Neelima, and then to me, 'By the way, where is Usha staying?'

'No idea,' I said. 'She didn't tell me, so my guess would be with some friend of hers, since she knows I will try to meet her at her aunt's or cousin's pad...'

We spoke for a long while, listened to some music, ordered Domino's pizza, and I felt quite light-hearted. I fished out some spare nightsuits and they just crashed in the guest bedrooms, having decided to pick up their stuff from the Ginger in the morning. Thankfully, they seemed to be supportive of me.

༠༠

I gathered that Neelima was seeing a guy from IIT Delhi who was about to take the GRE.

Bijlee, as usual, was keeping to himself, and was quite uninterested in the 'highly overrated hormonal interplay called pre- and post-marital romance.'

Arpita was seeing some guy at the commune but she added that 'he is too brainy to be my life partner, but too good-looking to be told so right now'.

None of them forced me to step out, as the media was just waiting for an opportunity to grill me with tough, unavoidable and uncomfortable questions. The watchmen used to call me up on the intercom to inform me that a few paparazzi were hanging around at a nearby tea stall, and were asking about the cars I owned.

The paparazzi were simple folk with simple plans. If any of my cars came out, they would tail it from a discreet distance, try to get some wide-angle photographs and sell them to the tabloids and mags.

I couldn't trust the watchmen either—they would have already taken some money to pass on some tidbits of information, and I knew that they were just calling me to con me into believing they were on my side. Probably, the watchmen were just checking if I was still at home. You couldn't trust anyone but old pals.

Anyway, I had no immediate worries, as I was certainly not going to step out in the near future and gift the paparazzi a field day. So we just chilled out at home for about a week. Neelima and Arpita managed the kitchen and the washing machines, while Bijlee and I did a bit of vacuum-cleaning every now and then. We watched lots of movies (some of them mine), played dumb charades and Scrabble and cards, and either ordered food or entrusted ourselves to Arpita's and Neelima's culinary skills, which were quite rusty, to put it mildly.

I wasn't complaining though, as I was beginning to feel less depressed. They wouldn't allow me to drink too much either, and just knowing that there were people who still loved me and cared for me, despite my obvious imperfections, made me feel infinitely better.

At the end of the week Arpita said we'd all be flying down to Bangalore soon.

'What for?' I asked.

'We have a plan,' said Arpita.

'C'mon, I am not going to Bangalore, and the pathetic paparazzi will be waiting for me at the airport anyway.'

'Listen, Vishy. Let us just do what Arpi says,' said Neelima.

'And what will we do in Bangalore? If you guys want a quiet holiday, then there is place called Dahanu...or even Alibaug will be okay...'

'Arre, don't talk nonsense, dumbo. This is not for us. This is for you,' said Bijlee.

'You mean, to make me happy and all?' I said. 'Let us just chill out here.'

'No, I have got the tickets, we are taking the early morning flight to Bangalore tomorrow...the 8 a.m. flight,' said Arpita.

'Arre, what for?' I repeated.

'Surprise!' said Neelima, and I left it at that, too tired to argue any further.

'Okay, I am game, but I don't wish to meet the bloody press hounds,' I said.

'C'mon, yaar, you are sounding as paranoid as Gene Hackman in *The Birdcage*,' said Bijlee.

'Vishy, we will leave in a fully-tinted Scorpio, I have arranged it, and even if they see you leaving and follow us, so what? They can't eat you alive—' said Arpita.

'And if they eat him, they will die of an overdose of alcohol,' observed Bijlee.

Nobody laughed.

Anyway, I wasn't taking any chance, so I called up the security cabin on the intercom at 6 a.m. and said that I was leaving for Pune in a short while. I was sure they would pass on the info to the media guys and the latter would follow the decoys. I had earlier called up a music director friend living two blocks away, late in the night, asking him to arrange two drivers for my cars.

The first driver took off in my Audi towards Pune at 6.05 a.m. I called him up in a bit, and he said that he was being tailed by a Qualis. Good.

The second driver took off in my Merc towards Nimika 's pad at 6.10 a.m. He called me up to say he was being tailed by a Maruti Swift and a Tata Indica. Great. The media hounds were being thrown completely off the scent. Hopefully.

I had instructed both the Audi and the Merc drivers to pull up the heavily-tinted windows, so that the media would think I was in there.

I think the media fell for the decoy manoeuvre.

The Scorpio drove us down to the airport at 6.20 a.m. I crouched on the floor at the back. Nobody tailed us. Nobody grilled me at the airport.

I fell asleep on the flight to Bangalore even before lift-off.

God only knew what we were going there for, anyway. Who cared? But it felt nice to be leaving Mumbai for a while, flying away from tragic memories of my recent past and from all the recent happenings that had rattled me beyond repair.

The Climax

Life is a prankster, magician and supplier
of high-voltage shocks.

'Where the hell are we heading to?' I asked.

'You will soon know,' said Arpita.

There was no point asking anything. Either these guys had a nasty surprise in store for me, or they were just planning a holiday at a resort or something. Nothing could be worse than what had already happened in my life, so nothing mattered anymore.

The car took a dusty road after we left the highway, and after a while I saw a signboard that said: Welcome to MOKSHA Commune. The acronym was explained below the name: Ministry of Krishna Service and Happy Atmas.

'What the bloody hell? I am not going to meet some guru-shuru and bullshit people like that!' I yelled.

'Vishy, stop screaming, we are not going to meet any guru. We are going to be with friends,' said Neelima.

The car parked at a huge gate and we alighted.

Two red-robed monks opened the gate and welcomed us in.

They both smiled at Arpita as if they knew her. She smiled back.

'Sorry, vehicles not allowed inside,' said the monk to all of us in general.

'Cool,' said Neelima. 'No problem.'

'Is he around?' asked Arpita.

'Of course, he is waiting for you,' the monk said to Arpita, and turning to me, 'I have seen some movies of yours, on TV, of course; you are a good actor.'

'Thanks,' I said. 'Whose commune is this?'

'You haven't told him?' the monk asked Arpita.

'No,' she smiled. 'We are giving him a surprise.'

The commune was impressive. There were a few people in red robes sitting in mediation in a huge garden full of flowers and trees. The living quarters beyond the garden, shaped like a semi-circle, were spread over two floors, and the buildings weren't painted at all—the outside walls wore a rock-like texture. The money plants and jasmine creepers cascading from the terrace lent the walls an old-world charm. I liked the natural simplicity.

We climbed the stairs and crossed a huge meditation hall on the second floor. I noticed that there were no paintings, no statues, no idols to be seen anywhere in the commune. I was already beginning to like the place.

The meditation hall opened into a huge terrace covered with bamboo awnings. At the far corner of the terrace was a dwelling that looked like the hermitage of some ancient sage. It was designed in the shape of a pyramid.

The monk stood outside the door and removed his footwear. We took the cue and removed ours, too.

'Come, please come,' said another monk who was waiting for us. 'Swamiji is eager to meet you all!'

When we entered the 'hermitage' I was struck by its bare simplicity. Wooden floors. Empty walls. Faint hint of frankincense. Cane chairs carrying red cushions. Soft breeze. That's all—nothing more, nothing less. It was compact and so very soothing. Obviously, this swamiji didn't believe in pomp and splendour.

'I will inform Swamiji of your arrival,' said the monk who had ushered us in.

After five minutes, Swamiji emerged from his room.

I was stunned! I was paralysed! I was shell-shocked!

This wasn't a surprise! This was a cruel joke!

'Hi, Arpi,' said Jana, hugging her.

Bijlee and Neelima namasted him.

'Don't look so stunned, Vishy. I am still the same old Jana,' he said, punching my shoulder like he always did. (I should have guessed it...they would conscript Jana to sort things out. But then, I had been too muddled to think logically.)

'Hell, no! I am so happy to see you,' I lied.

'Always the actor,' said Jana. 'Okay, guys, it is lunch time, let's go to the dining hall. We will catch up later.'

'This is just not done,' I whispered to Arpi as we walked towards the dining hall. 'You should have told me! I would've never agreed to come!'

'So now you know why you weren't told. And anyway, it is all for your benefit,' she said.

'What benefit? I am so uncomfortable meeting him. You don't know about the showdown we had when he couldn't crack a script—'

'Stop lying. I know all about how you manipulated Jana and Pavan, but Jana isn't small enough to hold all that against you. Grow up, Vishy. Put all that behind you, and start a fresh new chapter.'

'Damn you, Arpi! I am leaving soon!'

'Okay, after lunch!' she giggled airily.

༄

'Vishy, let's go to my room,' said Jana, throwing his arm around my shoulder affectionately as we exited the dining hall.

Arpita, Neelima and Bijlee left for the garden.

'Where are you guys going?' I asked.

'We have to meet someone, you guys carry on,' said Arpita.

'So Vishy, how are things? I guess you are doing well for yourself,' said Jana cheerfully.

'Hey, you aren't doing too bad for yourself, dude! Guru-shuru and all, huh? I heard you a few times on Omo, good stuff, bro,' I said, finding it difficult to pretend that nothing had gone wrong between us. (But then, I was a good actor, wasn't I?)

'Really? I am surprised. I thought you hated the "spiritual bullshit stuff".'

'Yeah, but I watched it because you were talking.'

'Cool. You know, when I talk, sometimes I think of the Burning Ghat and our long walks in Pune, and wonder if I made more sense then—'

'Yeah, we used to discuss so many things then...actually, it always used to be a monologue...'

'You bet! I didn't let you speak much, did I?'

'Well, every now and then I did get a chance to slip in a few points. By the way, Jana, I wish to apologize.'

'For what?'

'Hmm...now don't act dumb, it doesn't suit you... Obviously for the time I called you to do the script, and then I—'

'Forget it. That's all in the past, Vishy. One shouldn't dwell too much on past events. It ruins the present. There's a solid reason that causes any event, which we can't fathom. Neither was it in your control to prevent it, nor in mine to avoid it. You did something, I said something. We are even.'

'Don't you ever get tired?'

'Of what?'

'Lecturing.'

'Never. I was born to do just that,' he laughed as we entered his room.

'Wow!' I said.

'You like it?'

The room opened into a private terrace garden that also had a small pond with a few ducklings and swans gambolling in it. Plus, the room itself reminded you of the Burning Ghat. The walls carried life-size pictures of the river and us four (Arpita, Usha, Jana and I) sitting on the park bench at the ghat.

'Wow, you have pictures of us? And the Burning Ghat? I thought you wanted to drop the entire past and all?' I said on a note of wonder.

'Yes, but one shouldn't forget one's roots. You know, Vishy, there will never be anything like the Burning Ghat. I would love to go back and stay there again, but now it is just not possible—'

'By the way, how did you create this ashram?'

'I didn't. Actually, my guruji, Sri Siddhavarahananda, made it. But unfortunately, he attained maha samadhi last year. Ever since, I have been running the commune. There are two more, one in Switzerland and one in the US. Sometimes I need to go there too.'

'Whew! You are an international swami, huh? But you should be all over the dailies and mags, man! If I hadn't seen you on Omo, I wouldn't even have known about you. Your PR managers aren't doing a good job.'

'No, Vishy, I don't want any publicity. I was even reluctant to appear on Omo. But a few trustees kept pushing me and finally, I had to relent. Hope it is helping a few.'

'Cool. I am so happy that we met again, Jana, reminds me of old times!'

'Yeah, me too. Nostalgia is good fun, isn't it?'

'You bet! But Jana, if your guru was so rich, why were you living like a beggar at the ghat?'

'My guru and I split some four years ago, we parted ways on a spiritual technicality. Just before he died, he sent me an email and I met him. He said I was right, and should take over from him. And you know, Vishy, you can't grow under the shade of a huge tree. You have to leg it alone... By the way, there is something else I wish to talk to you about—'

'My affair? I know you wrote a mail to Usha, she showed it to me—'

'Oh, did she? Okay. Anyway, let's talk about your life.'

'What about it?'

'Obviously, you want to be with Usha again.'

'Of course, but after what Nimika went and did, Usha is pretty pissed off.'

'Is she wrong?'

'No she isn't, but you know, Jana, it was a one-off thing...I think I was drugged.'

'I know!'

'You know? Know what? That it was a one-off thing with Nimika, or that I was drugged?'

'Both.'

'How?'

'Nimika told me.'

'You talked to Nimika?'

'Yeah.'

'When?'

'Well, off and on.'

'That bloody bitch, she has ruined my happy life, Jana!'

'You don't realize how much Nimika loves you as a friend, Vishy.'

'Balls she loves me! She's after my money and fame—'

'No, I am not,' said a voice from the doorway.

I looked up.

Nimika? Yes, it was her! Oh, no! I hoped I wouldn't strangle her or something! Would shocks never cease this morning? This was the existential equivalent of electrocution.

'Sit down, Nimika,' said Jana, and she sank into a cushioned cane chair.

'What the hell is she doing here? She was here, Jana? And you didn't tell me?' I said angrily.

'She's been here for three days now—'

'Wow! I am so thrilled that you are on her side,' I said sarcastically.

'Well, as you know, I am always on the side of the truth,' explained Jana.

'Bull! But how did you get in touch with her?' I asked.

'Well, Arpi arranged that,' said Jana.

'You guys are scheming, double-dealing bastards! This girl, this bitch, has ruined my life! And you are talking to her and sheltering her? Usha is the only woman I've ever loved—you know that, Jana—this bitch has no business to be here! Throw her out right now!' I shouted.

'Calm down, Vishy, we are here to talk like civilized people—' said Jana.

'Civilized? What she did was worse than barbaric,' I yelled.

'Vishy, give her a chance. Hear her out, please,' said Jana calmly. 'Your anger is justified, I am not denying that, but let her talk.'

'Okay,' I said, suddenly becoming resigned.

'Vishy, I am so sorry,' said Nimika.

'Thanks a million,' I said. 'Your apology is as useful as a drop of water is to a thirsty man in a desert—'

'Please, dude, spare us your sarcasm,' said Jana, cutting me short, and reminded me of something we'd learnt at our call centre: listening skills.

'Listen, Vishy,' said Nimika, 'I obviously didn't want any of this to happen, but I didn't have a choice—'

'What the hell! You're talking as if someone forced you to do all this—'

'Have you ever made any enemies, Vishy?' interrupted Jana.

'Well, some, I guess. The extortionists, some political parties, some girls I rejected, some directors whose movies I refused to do... Perhaps even Bawa was angry that I turned down two scripts of his after my third... Hey, don't tell me Bawa is the brain behind this—' I said, wondering who all were after my ass.

'Okay,' said Jana. 'Let me rephrase that. Have *we* made any enemies, Vishy?'

'We? You can't make enemies, Jana. Everyone likes you, despite your shocking frankness,' I said.

'This was before you became a film star,' said Jana.

'Before? You mean when we were in Pune?' I asked.

'Yeah.'

'Hmmmm...enemies...I guess if we both have been collectively nasty with anyone, then it was only with that bastard Naveen—'

'Exactly!' said Jana.

'You mean...you mean...are you...are you serious?' I spluttered.

'Dead serious. Naveen Katyal did all this—'

'I don't believe it! You are inventing a story to save Nimika's skin. How does she even know him? Plus, how can she be innocent? She told the media I got her pregnant. She even leaked an MMS—'

'After Naveen blackmailed me,' Nimika said.

'Blackmailed you? How? When? Why?' I asked.

'Well, Vishy,' Nimika began explaining, 'I met this Naveen at a private party—he was a hotshot VP with some Even Stevens, a celeb management company, with huge contacts—and of course, I didn't know then that he was your earlier manager. We kept meeting at a few parties, and one night my tyre had a flat. I think he did that, too. So he dropped me back home and stopped over for a couple of drinks. I guess he spiked mine with some date-rape drug and took some lewd pictures of me. I mean, really lewd. I am stark nude in them and...and...' she broke off and began to sob.

'Oh no! Did he?' I said, looking at Jana.

'We have the pics. You want to see them?' asked Jana.

'No, no, if you say so, Jana, it must be so. Then what happened?' I asked, beginning to feel sorry for her.

'He used these to blackmail me later. He made me invite you over and took pictures of us together. I'm sorry, Vishy, I tried talking him out of it, but he wouldn't budge. He didn't even want money. He just wanted to get even with you. I didn't want to do it, but I also didn't know what to do, I was so worried. I wasn't thinking straight—' she broke off again, this time letting out a not-so-gentle wail.

'Nimika, don't relive it!' said Jana, wrapping her in his arms. 'It's over. Everything's okay now. Just relax while Vishy and I have a quiet smoke. Be back soon. Stay here.'

We stepped onto the terrace overlooking the garden.

'What the hell, Jana! Do you think her story is even believable?' I said. 'And what do you mean, everything is okay? I am positively fucked, man.'

Jana waved to some monk below, and the latter nodded and left.

'It is true, Vishy. Naveen had been planning to play merry hell in your life, if he could, for a while now. He used Nimika as bait. Perhaps we should have handed him over to the cops that night in Pune—' said Jana.

'Hey! But what if he tries something funny with Usha, too? She's all alone these days and who knows, perhaps he is stalking her or something—' I said worriedly.

'Now he can't harm you or anyone else, Vishy,' said Jana coolly. The same old mischievous glint that flashed in his eyes when he was ultra-pleased with himself was there now.

'Why can't he harm me? Because he feels this much is enough? No way! Naveen Kutta Katyal is one helluva sadistic and vindictive bastard, man, you know it! He won't rest in peace till I am buried eternally—'

'He's dead. So relax.'

'*Dead?*'

'Yeah, he died three days ago. He was just enjoying torturing you emo—'

'He's dead? How? And how are *you* so sure?'

'I killed him, Vishy. Well, not personally—I had him killed.'

My head began spinning. I was feeling so dizzy that you'd have mistaken me for a hyperactive roulette wheel. I leaned back on the parapet.

'You...you...I can't even imagine you as a murderer—'

'Well, tough times require tough measures. Naveen's car swung out of control somewhere in the Western Ghats as he was driving down to Pune one night. Perhaps you missed reading it in the newspaper. Just a small mention in the news-in-brief. Anyway, don't tell anyone this. Let the media think it is a nasty coincidence, if they ever find out that he was—'

'But...but...how did you manage it?'

'Well, let's just say Guruji had some pretty devoted disciples in the Mumbai underworld. This is all you need to know. And swear that you'll not breathe a word of this to anyone else, only our gang knows about it.'

'Of course not! Hell, man, we should at least tell Usha about it. This is the only thing that will clear my name. She has just vanished, dude. I think I will mail her! Her cell's switched off though—' I shouted excitedly.

'You don't need a cell to talk to me, dumbo!' said a familiar voice from the door that opened onto the terrace.

What the hell! Was it her? Oh, yes!

'Usha! Usha! Oh, Q2! I am so glad to see you!' I rushed towards her and fell sobbing in her arms.

'It's okay, sweetheart,' she said, ruffling my hair. 'I know everything now.'

We stood hugging there for a while. This was pure heaven.

'How come you are here? How long have you been here?' I asked her.

'I came yesterday. Nimika and I had a long chat. Jana wished to break things slowly to you, and also study your reaction, I guess,' smiled Usha.

'You bloody scheming bastard! Thanks, dude!' I said warmly, and hugged Jana tightly as my eyes misted over.

He had helped me get back my Usha! How could I ever thank him? I wept in Jana's arms, and he laughed gently, saying I was behaving like a child. But who cared?

'I also deserve a hug,' said Nimika, stepping onto the terrace.

I looked at Usha through a film of joyous tears.

'Do whatever, you have my permission,' said Usha, 'as long as you don't make her pregnant again!'

Oh no! Things had happened so fast that I had completely forgotten about that allegation!

'Vishy, I'm not pregnant. Naveen made me lie about that, too! Nothing happened between us that night. You were zonked, I wasn't. Usha knows about it—she's just joking. You never slept with me. But Naveen wanted to torture you emotionally. *"Just wondering whether he did or did not sleep with you will drive him crazy; just trying to remember that night, and knowing that he can't recall anything will fuck his mind!"* Those were Naveen's exact words. Nothing much happened. Except a bit of...but you already know that from the MMS...' said Nimika.

'Oh, thank God!' I said, and gathered Nimika in my arms. 'I am sorry I called you names, you have gone through so much, buddy, really sorry.'

'It's okay,' she said, pecking my cheek.

'Okay, Nimika, the media guys will be here soon. Brace yourself for some real-life acting, girl!' commanded Jana.

'What are you planning?' I asked.

'You will see. Sit in the command centre. You can see the show on CCTV,' said Jana.

'Are you going to say that she was being blackmailed?' I asked.

'Are you crazy? Use your brains for once. Nimika gets blackmailed into maligning Vishy. Blackmailer is killed. So who had the motive to bump him off? You and Nimika.

Naveen died in a car accident. It is filed as an unfortunate incident and no one is any wiser...' explained Jana.

'What if they find copies of Nimika's pics and my MMS on his laptop or something? Once they find that, the needle of suspicion will point towards us anyway,' I said worriedly.

'It's all destroyed, Vishy. His laptop, two CDs, flash drive, and even the file storage on the Internet, where he stored it—' said Jana.

'How do you know so much?' I asked.

'Our guys are meticulous. And even if someone does suspect anything, they have no shred of evidence to link you with it. I am safe, because I can't be traced back to all this. So relax. Don't think too much about it. We have worked out all the angles—' said Jana reassuringly.

'But he uploaded the MMS from his comp, right?' I said.

'No, he was smart. He logged in from a cybercafé, so for all intents and purposes, if the IP address is traced, it all came from God-knows-where in Goa. Thankfully, he didn't use Nimika's comp because—'

'Swamiji,' said a monk rushing towards Jana, 'the media has been waiting for ten minutes now, they are getting restless. Let's do this fast—'

'Yeah, sure, and take Vishy to the command centre,' said Jana to him.

Command centre? Where was I? At the Pentagon or at Langley?

I had slipped into a red robe and a monkey cap to escape media attention as we entered the command centre. Nobody recognized me. I was just another monk trying to attain nirvana, with the help of Jana.

All 20 CCTVs were switched on. They showed different parts of the commune. Obviously, there were hidden cameras monitoring the commune 24/7. So much for spiritual simplicity. Three CCTVs were trained on Jana.

Neelima, Usha, Arpita and Bijlee had also gathered at the command centre.

Jana was addressing the media in the open garden. The camera panned to Nimika, who was sitting far away from Jana. There was a cordon of monks around her who didn't let the media interact with her; they just allowed a few stills and videos of Nimika from a distance. No up-close interview. Yet.

What the hell! She had been looking drop-dead gorgeous just minutes ago! Now she looked totally down and out, morose, depressed and insane. What an actress!

'Well, thank you friends, for coming. Nimika wanted to make a statement, but as you can see, she is very disturbed by all the events that have occurred. A few psychiatrists are monitoring her. They say she is suffering from mental trauma and hallucinations, and should not be disturbed. So you can consider me her spokesperson for now. I will answer all your queries on her behalf,' said Jana.

'But Swamiji, what has happened to her?' asked a TV reporter.

'Well, let us just say it is a mental breakdown. That is all I can reveal—' said Jana.

'Does Nimika require psychiatric treatment?' asked a girl whom I recognized. She covered Page 3 for *The Bangalore Bioscope*.

'Absolutely,' said Jana. 'She's under medication even as we speak. Her psychiatrists have said she can either be here or they can admit her at their facility anytime, let's see what happens eventually. But they have assured us that she will recover, it is just a matter of time, nothing serious—'

'Does Vishy know about her condition, and what is he saying? Have you heard from him? I understand you are friends,' shot another media guy.

'Of course he knows. He has forgiven Nimika, understanding her underlying mental problem. I have spoken to him. Very kind of him to be so compassionate—' said Jana.

'Where is he? Why is he evading the media?' asked a svelte anchor.

'I know where he is but I won't tell you. Secondly, don't you think he will be embarrassed to face you guys after you have gone to town maligning him?' said Jana.

'But he and Nimika were…er, involved in a clandestine affair—' said *The Bangalore Bioscope* girl.

'Nimika says she drugged him that night—' said Jana.

'Is that her version?' asked an anchor.

'Yes,' said Jana, 'and she says she's feeling sorry for what she's done.'

'Swamiji, can we hear it directly from her?' asked a columnist.

'Let me see if she is in a position to talk to you guys. Stay here, please. Let me have a quiet word with her,' said Jana, moving towards where Nimika was seated.

He spoke to her for a minute. Then he escorted her back to where the media people were jostling each other to be the first to talk to Nimika.

'Calm down, please. Try to understand that she requires our love, sympathy and compassion at such a delicate phase of her life,' said Jana.

Most of the media nodded understandingly—and that was surprising, given that the media is usually as compassionate as Jack the Ripper when it comes to ripping apart celebs.

'Hello Nimika,' said someone. 'How are you feeling now?'

'Okay,' said Nimika softly. She seemed anything but okay. She looked mentally ill. Will someone please nominate her for an Oscar this year?

'Can you tell us all that happened?' asked an anchor.

'Well...hmmm...I apologize to Vishy and...and Usha, his wife, she's one of my best friends...for the trauma I have caused them—'

'But what happened that night?' asked *The Bangalore Bioscope* girl.

'Well, I mixed a date-rape drug in Vishy's drink, when he came over to my place—' said Nimika tiredly.

'Which one?' asked an anchor.

'Rohypnol,' said Nimika.

'You seem to know a lot about date-rape drugs,' sniggered the svelte anchor.

'Please,' Jana shouted at the anchor. 'Give her the respect she deserves for having the guts to speak out when in such a state...'

The svelte anchor was shushed by her colleagues.

'Yeah, I know about date-rape drugs. Last year I researched them as we were working on a script revolving around a date-rape case...' said Nimika.

'*Date Ka Rate*, right?' said a knowledgeable anchor.

Nimika nodded weakly.

'Anyway, nothing happened that night,' said Nimika.

'But you said you are pregnant with Vishy's love child?' observed an anchor.

'I lied,' said Nimika.

'Why?' asked a cub reporter.

'To put pressure on Vishy to marry me. I have always loved him,' said Nimika.

'So you did all this to break Vishy's marriage, hoping he would divorce his wife and marry you?' asked the svelte anchor.

'Yes, but it's all over now. I wasn't thinking straight—' said Nimika.

'This can get you into legal trouble, Nimika, you say you drugged him that night—' observed a reporter.

'No, Vishy is not pressing any charges against her. Don't stress her out. She's under heavy medication. Also, she has been suffering from manic depression for the past year. You can check with her psychiatrists on that. Obviously, she is hallucinating. In fact, the script she'd been working on casts her as a seductress, and she's confusing that story with her own,' said Jana.

'Have you ever seduced anyone else like this or was Vishy your only victim?' asked the svelte anchor.

'End of interview. I also have this to say: the MMS that's circulating is ancient. It's from a video shot for their second movie. Go check that with Bawa. Nimika didn't circulate that. Bawa says that some disgruntled technicians whom he and Nimika had fired earlier may have been behind it. Thank you all for your precious time. That's all for now, folks. Jai Hind!' said Jana, and whisked Nimika away, even as the media began its usual oh-my-god discussions.

I laughed contentedly. Jana and Nimika had left them so confused that they could only speculate, draw no definite conclusions, and then spin more yarns.

Page 3 headlines from the future played in my mind: *Nimika's story pregnant with lies/Is Swami Hasyavarahananda Nimika's latest catch?/Was Vishy date-raped?/Saint Vishy forgives Nimika/Vishy lies low; lover lies through teeth/Love-child a figment of imagination?/Nimika courts trouble?*

ॐ

We all gathered in Jana's room.

'That went well, didn't it? By the way, you guys don't know that Nimika did seek psychiatric help for acute depression a year ago here, on earlier trips to Bangalore,' said Jana. (I knew he was lying. He must have arranged some bogus psychiatric case history with some hospital to fit in with his game plan, but I let it pass. The others didn't notice his smug twinkle when he explained, but I did.)

'Yeah, then that will tally, but what about the legal angle? What if this gets Nimika into trouble?' asked Arpita.

'Nothing will happen. After a week, Vishy will do a press briefing and talk again about Nimika's acute psychiatric condition. Don't worry, there are many hotshot lawyers we know, they will bail her out, I have spoken with them,' said Jana.

'Don't worry, guys, we can handle them. The only angle we need to cover is Naveen, and only you people know about the blackmail thing; obviously, I will deny it if you folks leak it out—' said Nimika.

'Hey, why would we? Mum's the word,' I said, and turned to Jana. 'Thanks so much, dude, you have done so much for me. I don't know how I am ever going to repay you—' I broke off, as I became misty-eyed with gratitude.

'Yes, you can repay me,' said Jana.

'How?' I choked on the word.

'Well, for one, we all can chill out in Switzerland for a while. And then, you can be the best man at my wedding there!' said Jana.

'Wedding? You are planning to marry?' I asked.

'Hey, Jana, this is wonderful! Who's the lucky girl?' asked Usha.

'She might be here in this room,' said Arpita.

'You, Arpi? I never thought—' I said.

'Not me, stupid! You know that Jana and I are the best of friends,' said Arpita.

'Then, if Jana isn't planning to steal Usha from me...' (Usha slapped me on the wrist as I said that) '...and Neelima is hooked to some IIT nerd...then it must be...Nimika?'

'Absolutely,' beamed Jana.

'Oh, this is swell news,' cooed Usha.

Nimika giggled coyly.

'When? When did this happen, dude?' I asked.

'I proposed to her last evening and she has graciously accepted—' said Jana.

'He's lying,' said Nimika. 'I am the one who asked him first—'

'You both are Mrs and Mr Fraud. Don't try your cheap tricks with us, Jana. We are not the stupid media. Obviously Nimika must have proposed to you,' exclaimed Usha.

'And what will happen to your swamiji status and all?' I asked.

'What will happen? All know that I am a maverick swami. I drink, smoke and do everything a normal guy does. And I talk about God, too. In fact, getting married will ruin my business because most disciples are actually attracted to the rebellious, bohemian tag attached to me—' Jana said laughingly.

'So getting married to me will ruin your spiritual business? Then why did you accept my proposal?' pouted Nimika.

'Oh, no, honey, I didn't mean it that way—' began Jana.

We enjoyed the lovers' tiff that played itself out for about a couple of minutes.

'Vishy, you should write a book on all this,' said Jana to me.

'A book? Tell you what, I've been toying with that idea—' I said.

'Yeah? Good. You know you are a good writer, Vishy. Remember the diary you used to write in Pune? And the secret one about Usha that is full of love poems and essays on romance?' Jana teased me laughingly.

'Hey! You wrote a secret diary about me?' asked Usha. 'You never told me!'

'Q2, actually I began writing one when I met you—' I said, glaring at Jana.

'Why haven't you showed it to me?' asked Usha.

'Honey, it is private—' I defended myself.

'No, now there is nothing private between us. Where is it?' said Usha.

'In my bank locker,' I said. 'It is my most prized possession!'

'As soon as we reach Mumbai, you have to—' said Usha.

'Usha, demand it as a wedding anniversary gift,' interjected Jana.

'All right, all right,' I said to her. 'I will show it to you, honey, it is juvenile but that is okay, too, I guess.' And to Jana, 'But, dude, even if I write a book, I can't tell it all, can I, the stuff about Kutta Katyal's death...?'

'Arre, don't be a wimp. Just write it as fiction. No power on Planet Earth can link me with Naveen's death. But tell the world your story. It is interesting. So just do it, publish it, let people know what you went through, your rise and all that...' said Jana.

ॐ

Neelima, Bijlee and Arpita left that evening. Usha and I decided to stay back for a week. It is nice to gather the broken threads of a romance at a neutral spot, then return refreshed.

'You have a great friend in Jana, don't ever lose him,' Bijlee said as we bade goodbye.

'Never, Bijlee, and you are a great friend, too—' I said.

'Of course, but that guy has something special in him. You are a lucky guy, Vishy,' he said.

I nodded in agreement.

Jana was not of this world. He was a bit like a wise alien who had somehow dropped on Planet Earth. Despite my having turned nasty with him, he had not only forgiven me but also pulled me out of a very difficult situation. Plus, he had stuck his neck out to bump off Naveen. What had I ever done to deserve someone so special in my life? Anyway, it felt great to talk to Jana again and discuss philosophy and spirituality with him. There was lot of that happening at the commune actually, considering that Jana could break into a discourse anytime.

I felt Jana was back at Cosmos Callways—talking nineteen to the dozen—only this time around, his clients were devoted disciples, not the boring British; he was marketing God, not mobile phones; selling infinity, not infinite talktime. Otherwise, nothing much had changed. He was using the same sales techniques we had learnt at the call centre.

Even Nimika seemed more like Jana's student than lover. She gazed at him respectfully and listened to him intently.

'...even love is maya, pure illusion...' Jana had said yesterday at the evening discourse.

Whatever. Love may or may not be maya. Me, I was so much in love with my own maya, Usha, I really didn't care...

Epilogue

Xanadu Towers, 18th Road,
Bandra (West), Mumbai.
3 January 2012

Dear Reader,

Usha and I are now walking into a new chapter of life. Call it Take Two if you will.

I have promised myself that I will shower so much love on Usha that she will feel we are back in Pune, whispering sweet nothings to each other at Goratown Park.

Spirituality and God-consciousness are okay, but I'd rather be a devotee of maya than God. I know no God other than love. Also, I can't chase intangible things. I love my cars, my posh apartment, my celeb status, my bank balance and my wife—well, not in that order, not if Usha is reading all this!

We ushered in the new year at Shantanu's farmhouse in Khandala, where he also announced my next movie. Yeah, and I did finish my remaining scenes with him in just four days last week.

Nimika and Jana had flown down to spend the new year with us, so they were at the party, too.

The media 'friends' Shantanu had invited seemed quite disappointed about the patch-up, though. Magazines, tabloids and TV programmes sell because of juicy scandal, and the media hates it when a controversy fizzles out.

Ironically, the media is dismissing whatever happened as a publicity stunt for my forthcoming comedy movie, directed by Shantanu...which is on the subject of extramarital affairs in Bollywood! I did receive quite a drubbing from the media for staging this 'deplorable and pathetic publicity stunt', though. That I can live with. I am happy. So happy. Even Dad called up, wished me Happy New Year, and *almost* apologized for his earlier tirade. Naturally, I was feeling on top of the world. Usha's dad, too, wished me on the phone and invited us to Allahabad. We are planning to take a quiet holiday there in a bit. Perhaps we could spend Valentine's Day there.

No case has been filed against Nimika yet. Our legal eagles say they can handle anything, anyway. I guess the courts are pretty tired of celebs, their sordid lives and the meaningless tamasha surrounding them.

And so, our mega scandal will most probably die a natural death.

Funny, we never got caught when Nimika and I had really taken the media for a ride earlier, during the premiere of our first release; now, we are receiving flak for having spoken (part of) the truth. It just goes to prove that nobody believes you when you speak the truth and everyone trusts you when you spew lies.

I am not too bothered about my Friday fate, either. I have already made and invested enough money to lead a more-than-comfortable life. Dad is right, it is not money but contentment that decides the levels of one's happiness.

I have Usha with me. That's all that matters. Henceforth, I will live like a king. I will take risks, call the shots, do different kinds of scripts, experiment with my roles and meet Jana often to see if I am evolving like he says I should.

Oh, a word on marriage, too. Marriage is a wonderful thing. Real romance begins after marriage, actually.

Yeah, yeah, I know I was cussing that age-old institution a while ago, but you know how miserable I was feeling then. Misery makes you say nasty things—so never take the words of a miserable man or woman seriously.

Anyone who wishes to experience all the shades of love should get married. There is no other way. Life is meant for sharing, for caring, for finding divineness in togetherness.

I am feeling so *alive* today!

Well, almost. The kitchen is full of suffocating smoke that's making me cough, but I am enjoying it. Usha has gone to the beauty parlour, and I am going to surprise her by serving her Vishy-made pulao and potato curry when she returns in an hour or so.

I think I will wind up now with a few words of wisdom. *The way to a woman's heart? It's through her stomach...*

Take care. And do fall in love and marry and cherish your togetherness—it's worth it!

Yours sincerely,

[signature]

PS: One last thing. My story is true. The names in it aren't— yup, including mine and Usha's. So, keep guessing who we really are, if you have nothing better to do...

Acknowledgements

Vibhav, for all the booze, time, entertainment and clubbing

His wonderful wife, Geeta, the creator of groovy rajma

Anita and Ravi, folks who mistakenly think I'm interesting

Mukul, who generously wrote that blurb for *Campus Cola*

All my Facebook pals, for ideological tiffs and the 'likes'

Teji, for being that rare one who'll never read this book

My Chennai room, which still continues to tolerate me

My mom, who, quite surprisingly, does much the same

The Internet, without which I'd be a brain-dead ignoramus

For all guys who call me 'bro'; and for all girls who don't

Amrita, for mega patience and editorial support

The Rupa team, sharp minds that sculpt my works and being